HER DIRTY TEACHERS

MEN AT WORK BOOK 2

MIKA LANE

HEADLANDS PUBLISHING

BE THE FIRST TO KNOW...

Want more heat, heart,
and bad boys who know what they're doing?
Join my list and I'll send the steam straight to your inbox,
starting with a deliciously naughty story:

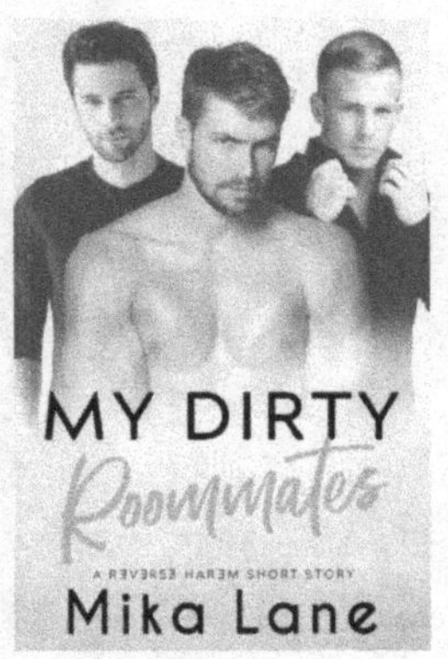

SIGN UP TO MY MAILING LIST!
Or visit:
https://geni.us/free-book-signup

1

SENNA DUNCAN

"Hey. See that guy back there? Third row?"

Godiva craned her neck around the stage curtain, straining to remain out of view of the audience. "I see about *fifty* guys in the third row."

I sighed and counted the number of tables. "Third from the front, second from the right. The guy in the black polo."

She squinted, too vain to wear glasses, and too squeamish to wear contacts. "Yeah. Oh. *Yeah.*"

I nudged her. "See what I mean? How come all our customers can't be like him?"

Rhetorical question. I knew the answer to that, just like Godiva did. It was a biological impossibility. Only so many men got the kind of good looks that make your breath catch. And your panties wet—if I were to be honest.

The universe was only so kind. The rest of us were allocated average looks. Not that I was complaining. It was just the way it was.

Thank god for flat irons, makeup, and gym memberships.

"He is quite something," she confirmed with a nod.

Taken individually, his features were not that special. The semi-mussed dirty blond hair, slightly large nose for his face, and brainy round glasses almost caused me to overlook him.

I admit it. When I had downtime at Club V, I checked out our male guests.

Actually, they were all male.

But when I looked at this particular guy a little longer, the outstanding planes of his face, not to mention his chin dimple, came into view. As if his face had morphed. And become beautiful. Like when you take a few steps back from an abstract painting and it somehow all makes sense.

His brow was strong. Prominent, if I wanted to be precise, extending over his eyes as if to cast shadows. His hairline was high but not too high—the perfect indicator that he was past adolescence but in no danger of losing his hair. His lips were pressed together somewhere between a smirk and an obligatory *yeah, I'm having fun* grimace, often seen on guys who'd been dragged in by their buddies to see some tits and ass for a bachelor or birthday party. The kind of guy who'd rather be at home watching sports or reading a book in bed.

Strip joints attract all sorts of customers. And when you'd worked at one as long as Godiva and I had, you could size most of them up in moments.

Yup, that's what we did at Club V. Provided tits and ass.

"Don't you ladies have anything better to do than spy on our customers?"

We whipped around to find Zin, the impossibly tall, red-headed, and crew-cut proprietor of Club V, scowling.

I rolled my eyes. "Zin, I'm not on for fifteen minutes. What the hell would you want me to do? Scrub the toilets?"

She narrowed her eyes at me, her way of warning me to *back off* with the smart-ass remarks.

It never worked.

I put my hands on my hips while Godiva nervously finger-combed her long hair.

She closed her eyes as if she were saying *serenity now*. "Look. Shelle just called in sick. Can either of you cover her shift? Please?"

She only added the *please* because she'd just scolded us.

"I don't think—" I started to say.

But Godiva drowned me out. "Sorry, Zin, can't do

it. My kid's at home with a sitter." She looked at her imaginary wristwatch. We didn't wear watches when we performed. "In fact, after my next set, I gotta head out."

So Zin turned to me, secure in the knowledge that I had no kids, boyfriends, husbands, or partners of any sort and that I could therefore be available whenever she needed me.

"Senna?" she asked.

I bit my lip, wishing I could turn her down just to fuck with her. But that wasn't an option. I needed the money and would have worked all night long if I thought I could've handled it.

I nodded, not looking at her. She needed to think I was doing her a favor and not the other way around. The last thing I wanted was to be in her debt. I didn't like being in anyone's debt. Owing people was messy. And I didn't do messy.

I adjusted my outfit, now riding up my ass, and pointed my toe as best I could in my clear, seven-inch platform heels. Their height was a strain on the ankles, so I was constantly exercising mine to keep them supple. The last thing I needed was to mess up my joints. I needed this job for at least a couple more years. Then I'd be on easy street. Well, semi-easy street.

Zin patted me on the back. "Thanks, Senna. I appreciate it. It's gonna be a good night, I can tell. You'll make some money."

And with that, she turned to find another girl who

she could assert her dominance over. She never let anyone forget she was boss.

Zin was a woman of few words and shared pretty much nothing about herself, but rumor had it she'd been a dancer at the club when she was quite young, and when the owner was murdered during a hold-up, she'd slipped right into his place as boss.

Some people even said she'd set him up to take over the club. If that were true, and I'm pretty sure it was, she was crazier than anyone thought.

"What do you think of my new outfit?" Godiva asked, letting the curtain fall shut, curtailing our spying.

I had to hand it to Godiva. She had some of the classiest stripper clothes I'd ever seen on someone who took it all off.

See, at Club V, some of the girls stripped down to nothing but their birthday suits, showcasing their shaved lady bits and breast implants. Others, like me, kept our stuff covered. We were no less sexy in my opinion—in fact, I thought keeping a little on was *more* sexy. But I didn't judge. More power to them for getting butt naked. Going that far just wasn't for me.

Like most of the other strippers, Godiva made her costumes. She'd find something cute at the store, take it home, and find a way to copy it and make it that much more sexy. And her latest creation was outstanding.

For my upcoming act, I wore what would be considered a very revealing one-piece bathing suit. It consisted of a little triangle over my crotch connected to a slightly larger triangle over my ass, and two strips of fabric wrapping from back to front, over my boobs, and tying behind my neck. Godiva, on the other hand, preferred the bikini style costumes. Easier to get off, she'd told me.

She did a little twirl, her ass cheeks jiggling just the slightest bit from her movement, barely covered by her new sexy and glittery chainmail bikini. She'd somehow found matching gold chain and strung it around her hips for a belly chain. When the rest of her clothes were off, this little accent would sparkle nicely in the bright stage lights.

"You look amazing. Was it hard to make?"

She slapped her palm to her forehead. "Totally. I had to use metal cutters for the chain."

So crafty.

Zin reappeared quietly. "You're on," she said to Godiva just as the DJ introduced her.

Godiva's face blew up in a gorgeous smile. She parted the curtain and disappeared into the bright lights.

2

SENNA

"Wow. Zin was right. This is turning into quite the good night," Godiva said when she got back to the dressing room all the girls shared.

She opened the little purse she took onstage for the tips she got at the end of a performance. The bills—mostly tens and twenties—had been stuffed so tight inside it that half came flying out, scattering all over the floor.

I bent to help pick up her cash, returning a small stack to her. Jesus. Maybe I should consider 'taking it all off.' It seemed that dancing in your birthday suit earned a shit ton more tips than what I got for keeping my stuff concealed.

But that was fine. I preferred a minimum of coverage. If it cost me, I was okay with that.

Godiva rushed to put her street clothes on to get home to her little boy. I had a few minutes to kill before I was due onstage.

"Hey," she said excitedly, "tomorrow's the big day, huh?"

Ugh. She had to bring that up.

I took a deep breath and nodded. "Yup. Should be interesting."

She put a hand on my shoulder and squeezed, her blue eyes a little tired now that she'd removed her false eyelashes and heavy makeup. "You're gonna knock them dead. I know it. You're at least as smart as all the other people who'll be in your classes."

Um, yeah. "Your words to god's ears," I laughed weakly.

Sadie, the girl on after me, sat at the dressing table opposite, finishing her own makeup. "Oh my god, Senna, that's right. You're starting college tomorrow, aren't you?" She jumped to her feet and gave me a hug, which I half-heartedly returned.

I wasn't a 'hugger.'

But I did appreciate the sentiment. For the most part, the other dancers I worked with, particularly Godiva, had become like family. I'd never had such loyal, supportive friends in my life.

And they were honestly, truly happy that I was

starting at Wellshire University tomorrow. I was also pretty damn thrilled, as well as mildly terrified.

"Hey, Senna, you're on," Zin said, poking her head into the dressing room.

I popped to my feet as fast as my stripper heels would let me, powdered my face one more time, and headed for the door.

"Senna, if you could do me a favor, I'd appreciate it," she said as she walked me to the stage.

"*Another* favor, Zin?" I teased.

She ignored my sarcasm. "There's a special guest, a tall, blond man in a black polo, who's here for his birthday. His buddies asked that you give him a little extra special attention."

A tall, blond man in a black polo? Oh yeah, I'd be happy to show him a nice birthday. No problem there.

"Okay, Zin. But now you owe me double," I fake-grunted.

She didn't need to know I was thrilled to dance for the object of Godiva's and my earlier affection.

I sauntered out onto the stage and grabbed the pole, not so much to writhe on on but to use as a kind of starting point. I nodded at the DJ, who began to blast one of my favorite songs to dance to—*Cherry Pie* by Warrant.

At Club V, we got to choose our own music. Godiva stuck with mostly Beyoncé and Rihanna. But I was a rock 'n roll girl, and that's what I danced to. The songs I chose were such a departure from what everyone else picked that when my music came on, it woke up anyone who was only partially paying attention. And that included the table with the handsome blond man.

I shimmied my way over the stage, being sure to use all the real estate the small platform provided, then danced to the edge of it. After some bumping and grinding, I did my signature dismount, which was essentially a forward somersault off the stage, where I landed upright on my feet.

Yup, I did that shit in my stripper heels.

I gyrated around the audience for a minute or two, being sure to make lasting eye contact across the room with the birthday boy, to let him know he was in for something special. He just smiled back shyly, something that always got my motor revving.

The cocky guys who sat back and made you work for their lousy one-dollar tips? They could pound sand.

But the modest ones who showed a degree of respect? Well, those guys made my heart go pitter-patter.

By the time I got to the birthday boy's table, I'd been flirting with him from a distance for a good ten minutes. He'd be nice and warmed up, possibly sporting a big hard on, and wondering why I'd singled him out. It was now time for him to receive my full attention and a birthday he wouldn't forget anytime soon.

But there was a problem.

Shit.

At closer examination, there were *two* tall, blond men in black polo shirts at the table.

I wasn't going to break the spell by asking any questions, so I randomly chose.

And of course I chose the one Godiva and I had been checking out.

I started by shaking my ass in his face, then moved to sitting on his lap. I removed his glasses and ran my hands through his already messy hair. When his friends started hooting and hollering, I knew I'd found the right guy.

He kept his hands to himself as per the club rules, but I put on a little show, touching and rubbing on him all I wanted.

His blond hair was soft and smelled of clean, basic shampoo. My hands found his hard chest and biceps, and he easily supported me when I bounced on and off his lap.

And his gaze was glued to mine the entire time. In fact, it made me kind of nervous. That *never* happened.

All too soon, my last song came on. I discreetly looked over at the DJ, who nodded, my signal to wrap things up.

I handed my new friend back his glasses. "Happy birthday," I whispered in his ear, then skipped back up to the stage for my final bow.

That's when the money came. I grabbed the small purse I'd left by the stripper pole, and began to scoop up the bills thrown onstage by our happy customers.

Birthday boy and his friends laid some cash on the stage, which I placed in my purse, mouthing *thank you*.

With a final bow, I was done. Fifteen minutes of work, and I was a couple hundred dollars richer. One more dance that night, and I'd be well on my way to having my tuition for next semester.

3

SENNA

"Oh my god, you got to dance for that hot guy, Senna," Godiva said, pulling on her jacket to leave.

"I know, right?" I gushed, still catching my breath. "He smelled so good."

She gave me a kiss on the cheek. "Good luck tomorrow, sweetie. Call me when you get a break. I want to hear all about it."

For a moment, my heart broke that Godiva wasn't joining me in my college adventure. She was at least as smart as I was, and I knew she didn't want to dance forever. Hell, it wasn't possible to dance forever. The best a girl could do was make as much money as fast as she could before she burned out, and save, save, save.

Some of the girls I worked with blew their money as fast as it came in, but not me. I had a plan and I was sticking to it.

"Talk to ya tomorrow, sweetie," I said, holding the dressing room door for her.

But just as she started to pass through it, Zin came flying in, almost knocking her over. "Senna. You danced for the wrong guy, dammit."

Huh? I didn't pick the right guy? Well, my chances had only been fifty-fifty.

She stepped closer to me. "You had one job to do," she spat.

Oh, no she didn't.

In my heels, I towered over her. "For your information, Zin, there were *two* men at that table who were tall, blond, and wearing black polo shirts. Your instructions should have been clearer," I hissed back.

Her face twitched. When it came down to it, *she* was the one who'd messed up. Not me.

Sadie, heading to the stage for her dance, patted Zin on the back. "Don't feel bad. I'm sure he still had a good birthday."

Zin glared at us all, turned on her heel, and left.

Godiva laughed and took off.

With time to kill before my next dance, I reviewed my first day's class schedule. I'd studied the campus map, circling each of the buildings where my classes were to be held and was pretty sure I could find my way around without any major mishaps. I could always hit up another student for directions, but I'd been warned during orientation that a favorite trick was to send lost freshmen in the wrong direction.

It was supposed to be funny. But it would piss me off.

My first class, Freshman English, was in Hobart Hall. Scrolling through the list of faculty, I looked for my professor. When I got to instructor for the eight a.m. class I'd registered for and saw my teacher, I dropped my phone on the floor.

My mouth also went dry and a gulp of water did no good.

Messed up my lipstick for nothing.

Shit. Where was Godiva when I needed her?

The dressing room door opened. Had she come back, perhaps because she'd forgotten something?

But it was Sadie, returning from her dance. "Hey, you're up soon, honey. Zin told me to get you."

"Um, yeah. Okay," I muttered, hand over my mouth.

I was going to be sick.

"Senna? Are you okay? Are you nervous about school tomorrow or something? You look awfully pale all of a sudden. I'm really sorry I couldn't take that extra shift tonight, and that you got stuck with it—"

She babbled on while I picked up my phone and looked at the English faculty again.

The dude I'd just given the special dance?

He was my English professor. Hobart Hall, eight a.m. Tomorrow morning.

4

PROFESSOR BENJAMIN "BENNO" ADLER

"Have I told you how much I fucking hate Mondays?"

Joanna looked up from her New York Times.

"It's not Monday, Benjamin," she clucked, putting her feet up on her desk and turning back to her paper.

Shit. She was right.

I invited myself into her office, just next door to mine in Hobart Hall. "Okay, well, have I told you how much I fucking hate teaching Freshman English?"

She nodded slowly, putting aside the paper and taking a sip of her coffee. "You *have* told me that. Probably a hundred times."

And I probably would tell her a hundred more.

She sighed. "Look. It's your turn. I did it last semester, and Don what's-his-name taught it the semester before. Just suck it up, Benno." She threw me the smirk that made her so awesome. Everyone needed a coworker who called them on their shit.

And she was right. It *was* my turn. But that didn't make it any easier. Some folks loved teaching Freshman English. *All those fresh minds! So much possibility! What a way to impact the college experience!*

Yeah, no.

Freshman English was one of the few courses at Wellshire that absolutely every student was required to take. There was no way out of it—no amount of high school AP courses or for that matter, begging, excused anyone.

Which made it one of the most hated classes at the school. I'd estimate that about seventy-five to ninety percent of the students in each class did not actually want to be there.

So did I like teaching a course to people who didn't want to be taking it? Where the majority of students just dialed it in, did the bare minimum of work, and looked at me every time class met with daggers in their eyes?

Hell no.

And Joanna was right, that teaching the course rotated through the English department. And she was right that it was my turn to step up. But that didn't mean I wouldn't complain.

Fuck, fuck, fuck.

"So what'd you do over the summer?" I asked.

She gestured toward a photo on her desk where she was nuzzling up to another woman. "Got married," she said defiantly.

"No fucking way. You and Molly tied the knot?"

She picked up the framed picture and smiled. A softness washed over her face that I didn't think I'd ever seen.

Wow.

"Sure did. We eloped. The families freaked, but we did what was best for us."

Was she getting tears in her eyes?

No way. Not Joanna.

I looked at my watch and saw eight a.m. looming large. I popped to my feet. "Well, I'm taking you out to lunch to celebrate. Actually, maybe dinner. Then we can drink with impunity. We are college professors after all. Aren't we supposed to be drunks?"

"I think you have one up on me in that category. I'm dry now. It was a condition of my marriage. Molly laid down the law, and I said okay."

Well, I'd be damned. Another drinking buddy bites the dust.

"Hey, Benno, before you go, how was your summer?" she asked.

Before I could answer, she nabbed me on the one thing I was hoping she wouldn't. But if she knew, that meant everyone at the university knew.

I was screwed.

"Tell me. What's it like having been voted *Sexiest Professor in the West*?"

There it was. The moment I'd been waiting for. Of course it was just a matter of time before someone brought up the latest absurdity that was my life.

And it was goddamn humiliating.

I hung my head. "I have no idea what I'm going to do with that one. It's going to bring me no end of trouble. I can see it now."

She dropped her head back, laughing. "You thought you already had it bad with the undergrad girls dropping their panties for you."

Joanna knew just how to push my buttons. Just what you wanted in a 'work wife.'

I rubbed my temples. It was too early for a headache to be circling my head like a hungry vulture.

"Look at it this way. It will only help your whoring ways." She knowingly narrowed her eyes at me.

I headed for the door, now late for class. But I didn't give a shit. Let the students sit for a few minutes.

"Joanna."

"Yes, Benno?"

"Fuck off."

I pulled her door shut behind me and jogged to class, Joanna's unruly laugh fading behind me.

5

BENNO

"Welcome to Freshman English," I bellowed as I arrived at the classroom that would be mine for the next, agonizing, sixteen weeks.

Saying the very words made me want to puke.

I threw off my jacket and pulled some items from my satchel while I surveyed the class.

As usual, the front row was full of pretty, young girls with crossed legs under their short skirts. The back was strung with the typical too-cool-for-school kids who were laughing and joking with each other, comparing notes about their fraternities and sororities. The middle section was a mixture of both—the students who were actually interested in Freshman

English, and the ones too polite to show that they weren't.

As I surveyed the motley crew that was mine for the next semester, I noticed some tittering going around the room.

I put my hands up to silently ask the class *what's going on?* That's when one of the girls in the front row pointed at the blackboard behind me.

The blackboard I'd failed to notice when I'd entered the classroom.

"Um, Professor Adler—" she'd started to say as I turned around.

And there it was. Already starting.

Someone had scrawled on the board *Sexiest Professor in the West*.

It had really just been a matter of time.

But that didn't keep me from wanting to kill someone. I'd be a good sport about it, though.

What choice did I have?

I smiled, picked up the eraser, and stopped. Fuck all. I was going to leave it there.

I scanned the room of thirty-some-odd people. "You all got me. Yup. I'm the sexiest professor in the West."

Laughter swept through the room.

Awesome. I had them now. Cool guy who could take a joke. No problem. That was me.

Fuckers were going to feel the pain when they

found how hard I planned to grade them. Not that I was vindictive or anything.

"Okay people, starting in the corner here," I said, pointing to the first row, far left, "tell us your name and what your favorite book is."

As the task worked its way down every row, the students responded with the usual just-out-of-high-school fare—*The Call of the Wild*, *Twilight*, *The Hunger Games*, *Lord of the Rings*, etc.

It was so predictable I could have told *them* what they liked reading. Not that there was anything wrong with those books. I just wished high schools had a little more variety.

A young woman named Mabrie was introducing herself, explaining that she was from out of state and that it had been her lifelong dream to attend Wellshire, when the classroom door flew open.

A tall, buff guy breezed in.

Wearing a letterman's jacket and an insufferable smirk.

Every semester had an asshole. Guess this one was not going to be any different.

"Yo," he said in a deep baritone, "sorry I'm late."

He wasn't sorry.

A titter ran through the girls in the front row, who pulled back their shoulders and straightened up in their seats, straining to see where he was going to sit.

Jesus.

"Glad you could make it. Please grab a seat, introduce yourself, and tell us your favorite book."

"Sure, Professor," he sang, grabbing a seat in the middle of the room, I supposed so he could enjoy maximum female admiration.

At least it took some of the pressure off me.

"Hey, y'all," he began, looking around the class like they were his subjects. Which I guess they were, evidenced from the admiring gazes. "Most of you guys probably know me as Ty Duvall. I'm on the football team, for those of you who don't know who I am."

He acknowledged the nodding heads in the room, and ignored the eye rolls. Someone muttered *douchebag*, but if he heard it, he ignored it.

Then he turned back to me. "As for books... I've never read one."

A snicker ran through the room, and someone in the back combined a cough with a loud *bullshit*.

My sentiments exactly.

"Never read a book, Ty?" I asked, approaching him slowly. "Not even one?"

He leaned back in his chair, legs sprawled in the aisles. He tilted his head and looked up at me. "Nope. Not a one. You got a problem with that?"

Keep it cool. Keep it cool.

"I don't have a problem with that Ty," I said, placing a hand on his desk and leaning close to him. "But you're about to have a problem with that."

A momentary scowl passed over his face, quickly replaced by another smirk.

"Sure, Prof. Whatever you say."

I wandered back to the head of the class. "Let's continue."

I was flipping through my papers when the next person took her turn.

"Hi. I'm Senna Duncan. My favorite book is *Of Human Bondage* by Somerset Maugham."

My head snapped up in the direction of whomever had said that. No one ever said Somerset Maugham. I figured he just wasn't taught in school, if he ever had been, and that few kids picked up his work on their own.

As I looked around for the student whose favorite book was also mine, a gut-punch unlike anything I'd experienced in a very long time traveled through my abdomen. If I hadn't been in front of a class of thirty, I might have winced. Instead, I casually put a hand on the desk in front of me to play it cool.

"Well Senna. That's my favorite book, too. In fact, I have a signed copy. There's a bookstore down on University Ave that carries special editions. You should check it out."

She took her seat and looked down, writing in the notebook on her desk.

But it was too late to hide her face.

It turned out that my fellow Maugham lover was

the very same woman who'd given me the lap dance of
a lifetime just the night before.

6

SENNA

College sure was off to a great start.

My English professor, whom I'd shaken my ass in front of less than twenty-four hours earlier, recognized me without any trouble. It was written all over his beautiful but horrified face. Yup. While I stood there droning on about my favorite author, he was probably remembering the freckle on my left butt cheek.

Not how I'd expected my first day to go.

When the fifty-minute class let out, I burst to the front of the stampede making for the door to get the hell out of there.

If that weren't bad enough, in my next class, math, I had no freaking idea what my teacher was talking about. It was light years away from the algebra of my high school, which had been a long time ago, anyway. On top of that, he'd given out homework on the first day. I thought teachers never gave homework the first day.

And—there was more—it was time to report to my 'work-study' job, a requirement of the small amount of tuition relief I'd finagled out of the university. It didn't matter that I had another job outside of school. As part of my agreement, I owed them six to ten hours of my life each week, for which I'd be reimbursed at the rate of minimum wage.

The financial aid counselor I'd seen had said I could either take a job at the campus dining hall or the fitness center.

I couldn't believe he even had to ask me. Who the fuck would want to work in a dining hall?

So there I was, at the fitness center, which was abuzz with classes like CrossFit and tennis, as well as the school's athletic teams, and students and faculty alike arriving for their workouts. How bad could it be?

My supervisor, Patti, showed me to the front desk, where I was to scan the university ID badge of anyone who entered.

That was it. All I had to do was scan badges. Deadly boring, but there it was.

"Oh my god, that pink lip gloss looks so good on you," some girl cooed to her workout buddy while I scanned their IDs.

"Ugh," her friend responded. "I had an extra, which I'd give to you, except my bitch roommate stole it…"

Their voices got lost as they were swallowed by the clamor of the cavernous gym.

That was a first.

I'd never seen anyone work out in full-on makeup. But I guess I couldn't really talk. My regular workouts, which consisted of dancing at Club V, required heavy stage makeup. High intensity stage lights were not kind to the complexion, but we were still required to look our best.

"How's it going so far?" Patti chirped after I'd been on the job fifteen minutes.

I smiled with enthusiasm. If I didn't make this job work, I'd end up at the dining hall. And *that* would be a problem.

"Great, Patti. Thanks for asking."

She hovered for a moment while I scanned the badges of a couple lacrosse players. "You know, you can take any of the classes offered here, since you're working for the center."

I decided not to tell her about my 'regular job,' where I got a better workout than I'd ever get in some gym.

She seemed like she really wanted to talk. "Good to know. Are you taking anything?" I asked.

She looked around and lowered her voice. "I am. We have a brand-new burlesque dance class. Can you believe it? It's so sexy."

Cripes. I probably could have taught it.

I nodded with wide eyes. "Wow. That's really cool. I expected you to say something like racquetball."

Jesus. If she only knew.

Just prior to Club V, I'd been working a low-paying job at a day-care center. The only good thing to come out of that gig was realizing I was pretty sure I never wanted kids. Otherwise, I had constant colds from wiping the rugrats' snotty noses, and was always being hit on by the single—and some not so single—dads.

I was barely making my rent, and plans for anything better were sorely out of reach, until I talked to my neighbor, Godiva.

"Why don't you come down to the club? See how we do things there?" she'd suggested after I'd had her and her son over one night for some mac 'n cheese. *Boxed* mac 'n cheese.

Was she fucking kidding?

"Oh no, I couldn't be a stripper. For one, I'm a shitty dancer, and for another, I just don't know that I could drop trou for a roomful of strange men."

She looked at me patiently. "Well, you don't have to get naked, you know. The owner, Zin, likes to mix up the acts she books. Ya know, some full-on nudity mixed in with a more go-go vibe where you wear a sexy bikini or lingerie if you want. You've got a rocking body. They'd love you."

Me? A rocking body? Dancing nearly naked?

But it was when she told me how much money she made that she really got my attention.

In five years' time, Godiva had told me, she planned to retire *and* have enough money for her little boy's college education. She'd still work doing something low-key, maybe as a salesperson at Crate and Barrel or something like that, but she'd really be set.

And I was sold.

However, because I wasn't getting completely naked, and because I was the club's newcomer, I learned I'd only get a couple shifts a week. But the potential was there. I said goodbye to the daycare center and bought some sexy new outfits.

As she watched people come in and out of the gym, Patti's eyes suddenly widened. With strange reverence, she stepped aside to make room for none other than Ty, the jock from my English class who'd admitted he'd never read a book.

Who did that?

"Hey," he exclaimed, shaking his head at me like we were buds. "We have a class together. What'd you think of that dick professor? Christ, does he have a stick up his ass."

Ty looked at his friends who, following his lead, cracked up like he'd said the funniest thing ever.

Shit. Were these the kind of people I'd have to deal with every time I worked here? The dining hall was beginning to look better. I might have to wash dishes or something disgusting like that, but I wouldn't have to talk to anyone.

"Yeah, I'm in Professor Adler's class. I think you sat next to me," I said in a flat voice, not looking up while I scanned each of their cards.

Patti, meanwhile, was about to have a heart attack that a football player was chatting me up.

She could have him.

With his friends heading for the men's locker room, Ty moved closer to me. Patti took the hint and made herself scarce.

"Hey, why don't you take a spin in my convertible with me sometime?" he asked.

I choked on my Diet Coke.

I almost felt sorry for him. Almost. He had no idea what a cliché he was.

But I reminded myself to not be a bitch. I didn't bother to tell him I saw men with nice cars all the time.

And, I might not have my own fancy vehicle, but at least I wasn't a fool who admitted out loud he'd never read a book.

I looked around, wishing Patti would come back. "Thanks, but that's not really my thing."

He raked a hand through his dark hair, his eyebrows knit in confusion. "Right. Gotcha. First week of school is pretty busy. All right then. I'll hit you up in another week or so."

What? Was he deaf? Was he actually was so conceited it didn't register in his little brain that there was a woman not interested in spending time with him?

He wandered off, all confidence and cockiness. I sat and scanned ID after ID.

My shift was ending, thank god, when my replacement came. He smiled at me resignedly, settling into an on-campus job that he probably would rather not have, just like me.

"Hey, Patti. I'll see you Friday, okay?"

She jumped up from her desk. "Yeah, right. So glad you've joined the team, Senna."

As I clocked out, I saw Professor Adler enter the gym with a backpack on his shoulder, accompanied by a beautiful woman. She could have been a student, but I wasn't sure.

As the Sexiest Professor in the West, he probably had women hitting on him all the time. Even without that tribute, he was probably besieged by women anyway, he was so stunningly perfect.

I waited for him to pass through the badge scanner, and then sneaked out so he wouldn't see me.

· 7

SENNA

I HAD SOME FIRST DAY HOMEWORK TO GET HOME AND tackle, but I first wanted to check out the bookstore Professor Adler had mentioned, the one with the special editions. I really had no idea what he was talking about—wasn't a bookstore just a bookstore?— but he'd grabbed my attention with the promise of some sort of next-level literature. Like it wasn't enough to own my old tattered paperback copy of a Somerset Maugham book. If I were a real fan, I'd find one that the author had actually touched at some point in his life.

Plus, I guess I wanted to impress him by telling him I'd casually happened by the shop, as if I went there all the time.

I could see it now.

Oh, I was in Thidwick's yesterday. They just received a very rare edition of a Maugham book. I'm considering getting it. What do you think?

Yeah, right. Like he'd believe that.

And why did I care what he thought of me, anyway?

I didn't even have to think about the answer to that question.

I wanted him to regard me as more than a go-go dancer. I wanted him to think of me as smart and well-read, something not many people saw me as.

My mother had told me not to go to college. My high school teachers told me I'd never make it. Even my guidance counselor had told me not to bother taking the SAT—that it was a waste of my time.

I hadn't been the best student. And I might have been suspended for smoking and fighting.

A few times.

But there weren't many things that motivated me like naysayers.

I'd show them all, including Professor Adler.

"Hello. May I help you?" a high male voice asked from behind me.

Holy crap. Now this was a bookstore. It looked like something out of freaking Harry Potter. Right down to the elderly gent offering assistance. He was actually wearing a tweed vest and wire-rimmed glasses.

"Oh. Hello. My English professor told me about this shop, so I wanted to see it myself."

I headed down the main aisle and when I stopped at a row called *British Authors*, I realized the clerk was right on my tail.

"Oh. Excuse me," I said when I bumped into him.

"Perhaps if you tell me what you're looking for," he said, looking me up and down, "I can save you the time of wandering about."

I shook my head, displeased by his once-over. "Thanks. I'll let you know if I need anything," and I started to walk away, charmed by the slight musty smell and dark bookshelves towering all the way to the ceiling.

"Miss, I don't think we have anything for you," he said stiffly.

I whipped around. Was he giving me a hard time? I was a fucking customer.

"Do you have a problem, mister?" I asked, taking a step toward him.

You can take a girl out of the neighborhood, but you can't take the neighborhood out of a girl.

His eyes widened, and he took a step back, clearly not expecting me to call him out. But he double-downed anyway. "We don't have anything for you."

"How would you know? I've not even told you what I'm interested in—" I started to say.

But when I realized the way I'd dressed, in jeans,

thigh-high boots, and a fringed leather jacket, had allowed him to pass judgment, it all became clear.

"I see. You don't want me here because I don't look the way you think I should."

Memories of those who'd doubted me came flooding back, accompanied by a creeping insecurity I thought I'd shaken off.

Fucker.

I turned on my heel, brushing against him as I made for the door. I wouldn't normally let such a little weasel chase me away, but I was fighting off tears that I couldn't risk the asshole seeing. I bolted out of the dark shop into the last of the day's sunlight, and even though the sun was low, I pulled on my sunglasses.

With a couple deep breaths, I'd halted the threatening tears. I was good at it. I never let myself cry.

8

PROFESSOR JAMES "JAMIE" CARTER

"Dude, what is it about academic life? I always feel like I'm getting fucked in the ass."

I waved the bartender over. I needed another beer. "Two more Stellas," I said, throwing a twenty on the bar.

"What's up? Same old crap?" Benno asked.

I looked at my friend, known to his students as Professor Benjamin Adler. He'd climbed up the academic ladder like it was made for him. Published his English papers to great acclaim. His students loved him. And he'd just been voted Sexiest Teacher in the West or something stupid like that.

Which irritated the hell out of him.

My journey through the academic world had been much bumpier. One step forward, two steps back. My latest challenge was, plain and simple, that the head of the department where I taught was not a fan of mine. But in fairness to him, quite a few people weren't fans of mine. Nor of my family.

That's how things went when your dad was an embezzler of epic proportion, whose misdeeds cost hundreds of people their life savings and even retirement. And as his son, and former second-in-command of his now-defunct financial advising firm, people assumed I was just as evil.

I wasn't.

But thanks to the old *guilt by association* thing, I was fucked.

My mom had called me one rainy New York morning about three years ago, crying, "Your... your father has just been taken into police custody."

I'd been in a cab, navigating Manhattan rush hour traffic in shitty weather. The windows were steamed up on the inside, and the driver smelled like cigarettes.

"What, Mom? It's hard to hear you. Can I call you when I get to the office?"

But calling her from the office never happened. I arrived to a chaotic shit-show of FBI, police, and the District Attorney's office swarming the place, with the last few remaining employees packing the little they were allowed to take before hitting the road.

My life changed that day. But not as drastically as the lives of the people my dad had ripped off.

I must have been asked a thousand times, *how did you not know?*

And I've answered a thousand times, *I wish I had.* I really did. He'd hid it from me. Sure, other executives in the company knew of my dad's scheme. It wouldn't have worked without them. But I hadn't known a damn thing.

Dad would take money from new, unsuspecting investors, and when he lost their money in the stock market, he'd just lie and pay them with investments from other new, unsuspecting investors. A pyramid scheme in the truest sense.

I knew nothing, and my innocence was eventually proven. But by that time, my reputation was shit. My friends and colleagues, for the most part, had bailed on me.

See ya.

It was the end of my life as I knew it.

So I left New York.

I'd always been curious about being an educator, so I started as a teaching assistant at Wellshire University and worked my way up to associate professor. I was enjoying teaching math, my favorite subject, when a new boss joined the department. He didn't like me. Not one bit. He knew all about my father's company and how people had been swindled. He was convinced that if I'd had nothing to do with it, then I at least must have known what was going on.

I was guilty in his eyes and always would be.

So my full professorship was lagging. Actually, it was more like dead in the water. I was losing hope it would ever happen.

"I mean, what does one do when you're passed over for tenure?" I asked rhetorically.

I already knew the answer, but Benno decided to clarify it for me.

"You can stay and just hang in there, or you can leave. Go to another school, or do something else altogether. Sorry, man."

I needed to stop bitching before I ruined the night.

"So what's going on with you, Sexiest Teacher in the West?" I asked, slapping my hand on the bar and laughing my ass off.

"Fuck off. And if you must mock me, get it right. I'm the sexiest *professor*, not teacher."

I fake-gagged. "How'd you get picked for that, anyway?"

He threw me his serious stink eye. I knew he hated the attention, but it was funny as hell. There was no denying it.

He shook his head. "Dunno. I guess someone nominated me and they picked me. I wouldn't mind finding out who did it, though, so I could punch them in the mouth."

"Dude, get over yourself. It's funny, not the end of the world."

He looked down at his beer and shook his head. "No man. It's embarrassing as hell. In my first class yesterday, some joker wrote it up on the board. I didn't even notice until the students pointed it out."

"Well, I ain't crying for you."

Benno's face turned serious. "Hey, Jamie, I have to tell you the craziest thing."

Anything to get my attention off the university, and my stalling career.

"You know how there was that birthday party thing for that guy in my department Tuesday night?"

I nodded. "Yeah. That new guy, right?"

"Yeah. We had beers and then ended up at Club V afterward. He'd never been. I didn't really want to go, but all the other guys did, so I figured what the hell."

I shook my head. I hadn't been able to stop thinking about it all day.

"So, there was this dancer who paid special attention to me. Freaking amazing, stunning woman. At first I couldn't figure out why she was focused on me, shaking it in my face and all that, until she finished and whispered 'happy birthday' in my ear. She'd danced for the wrong guy—"

"No, she danced for you because you're the sexiest professor in the West!" I blurted out. I couldn't help it.

He scowled but continued, lowering his voice. "So get this. My freshman English class meets for the first time. I'm tired and cranky, pissed that I have to waste my time with a bunch of kids who couldn't give a damn, and who's in my class but this woman? The one from the club." He slammed his hand on the bar for emphasis.

"The one who danced for you?" I was incredulous.

Why didn't things like that ever happen to me?

He shook his head in disbelief. "It was one of the weirdest fucking things to ever happen to me. There she was, of course with more clothes on this time, but no less beautiful. I nearly fell over. I literally had to hold onto my desk."

I guessed something like that was inevitable when you lived in a college town. But it would be weird nonetheless to stand up in class and look directly at the very woman who'd given you a boner the night before. If you weren't expecting it, anyway.

"And want to hear something even crazier, Jamie?"

"Um, what? She stayed after class and gave you another lap dance for an *A*?" I laughed.

"Very funny. She's a reader. We were going around the room, with everyone introducing themselves and saying what their favorite book was. Hers, it so happens, is the *same as mine*."

He drummed his fingers on the bar with a dreamy look on his face. Christ, something about this woman had really gotten under his skin.

"Good god. What are the chances?" I said, shaking my head.

What a crazy coincidence.

And *now* I knew why she was getting to him. He was a sucker for a well-read woman. Stripper or not.

He nodded, clearly still blown away. "In all my years of teaching, no one has ever claimed a book by Somerset Maugham to be one of their favorites. Not once."

I waved the bartender over for the check. "Much less a *stripper* claiming a book by Somerset Maugham to be her favorite."

Benno reached for his wallet, but I stopped him. "You got the last round. This one's on me. Drink up."

He took one last swig of his beer. "Why are you in a hurry all of a sudden, Jamie? Do you have somewhere to be?" he asked.

I grabbed my bag and jacket. "Get your stuff. We *both* have somewhere to be."

9

JAMIE

"No fucking way, Jamie. We are not going to Club V right now. It's late and besides, it would be a dick move to spy on this woman," Benno insisted. "She's my student for Christ's sake."

I steered my Land Rover onto the club's crunchy gravel parking lot and chose a spot in the far corner, where no asshole could put a ding in my car.

"C'mon. Just for a couple minutes. I want to know who she is," I begged.

Benno shook his head. "She's probably not even there." But he got out of the car anyway, grumbling, "This is such bullshit."

Not two minutes later I'd paid the cover charge and

selected a table as far in the back of the club as possible. I waved a scantily clad waitress over for a couple beers. I was tempted to go for something stronger like tequila shots, but I didn't want to push Benno off the deep end.

I looked around the place. It really wasn't that bad for a strip club. And the dancer onstage at the moment was stunning.

"Is that her?" I asked.

He shook his head.

"Hey, Benno, I've been meaning to tell you," I said, leaning toward him to be heard over the pulsing music. "I have a business idea."

"What's that?" he bellowed.

"If I don't get my professorship, I may open a bar."

He looked at me like I was crazy. As I'd expected he would. He was a cool guy and one of my best friends, but thinking outside the box was not something many college professors usually did.

They didn't have to.

I held my hands up. "Hey, don't dismiss the idea outright. You know I have the funds to do it. I've toyed around with the idea for years."

"How much do you think it would cost to get it up and running?" he asked, his 'you're crazy' look fading slightly.

"Couple hundred grand to make it nice."

Benno knew my situation. He was one of the only people who did, and certainly the only person at the university who did, besides our friend Chase. My dad may have gone to prison and forfeited his assets, but they didn't go after mine, and being a financial advisor in New York was pretty freaking lucrative. Truth be told, I didn't need to work another day in my life if I didn't want to.

The key phrase was *if I didn't want to*, because of course I wanted to work. I wasn't one of those rich pricks who sat around and pretended to be busy all day really doing nothing.

Like a few of the supposed friends I'd left behind in New York.

"Are you going to do it?"

I sat back in my seat and shrugged. "Maybe I will—"

But I stopped short when I saw the expression on his face.

Was it her?

A hard-driving rock 'n roll song started blaring, and the most stunning woman I'd seen all evening skipped out onto the stage wearing a glittery bikini top, Daisy Duke shorts, and a wide Western belt holding them up. She'd accessorized herself with a cowboy hat and some matching high-heeled cowboy boots.

From the expression on Benno's face, it *had* to be her.

And she was goddamn awesome.

She twisted and turned on the stage, tossing around what I figured was a long blonde wig, playfully engaging with the guys in the front and second rows.

Then, she did the craziest flip off the stage and started working the floor.

"It's her, isn't it?"

But Benno had grabbed his jacket and ducked as if to hide his face. "My Uber is here. Talk to you tomorrow."

"Okay. Suit yourself," I said, settling back into my seat while he headed for the door.

Benno's little dancer was making her way toward my side of the room, just when her song wrapped up to huge applause. She smiled and bowed when I realized something.

She was not only in Benno's English class. She was also in my math class.

10

SENNA

"I'LL NEED TO SEE A COPY OF YOUR CLASS SCHEDULE."

I passed a piece of paper to Krishelle Abalone, my assigned academic advisor, and from what I could tell so far, a very unhappy person.

As soon as she ran down my list of classes, she stiffened.

Was there something objectionable about the three classes I'd signed up for? Did she think I ought to be carrying a heavier load? Because I had every intention of adding one more class as soon as I figured out which to take.

"One of the things I wanted to ask you about, Krishelle—"

"It's Ms. Abalone," she interrupted.

Really?

"Right. Ms. Abalone," I repeated, hoping she'd hear how absurd she sounded. "I'm interested in adding a fourth class."

She just kept frowning at my schedule.

"Um, is something wrong?" I asked.

She signed deeply. "Well. It's just that you have Adler for English."

Oh my god. Did he tell her he'd seen me at Club V? Was she gathering ammunition to shame me? Because if she were, I was going to give it right back to her. Possibly with my fist.

On the other hand, if her thinking was that he was a shitty teacher, maybe I could move to another class. Preferably one where the professor hadn't seen me mostly naked.

"Is he a bad teacher or something?" I asked.

Ignoring my question, she pointed at the schedule. "I'm glad to see that you've chosen a 'coast' class. You're going to need that."

It was true I had a class that seemed like it wouldn't be too challenging in order to balance out the other, harder ones I'd be taking. But her pointing it out was pretty bitchy.

"And why do you say that?" I asked.

"Well," she said, looking me up and down.

What was it with the people at this fucking place, always looking me up and down?

"You're going to need it. Expect to be very challenged this semester. If I were you, I might not even add a fourth course."

"Why is that, Ms. Abalone?"

She pursed her lips, clearly looking for the right words. But there really weren't any right words when you were insulting someone.

"Let's just say, Senna, that a student of your abilities needs to proceed with caution."

What? Did she just say what I think she just did?

A nasty heat washed over my face, and I knew I was turning deep red, especially when Abalone's eyes widened and she sat back in her chair, like she was afraid I was going to punch her.

Couldn't blame her. I would have loved to have a go at her. But the survival tactics that worked in the rough neighborhood where I'd grown up didn't really translate to a university setting.

"A *student of my abilities*. I'm wondering what you mean by that?" I asked, practicing all the restraint I possibly could and then some. Sure, she'd seen my transcripts, but I'd taken extra classes to get into the university. I'd been admitted because I was qualified.

She turned to her computer and typed in some notes. "You don't seem to be the best-prepared student the university has ever seen," she said, turning back to me with an awfully satisfied smile.

Oh, to wipe that ugliness off her face…

"What are you majoring in?" she asked to change the subject.

Fine. The bitch could change the subject. But I wasn't going to forget her assumption.

"I've always loved reading, so I was thinking of majoring in English. But if you think Alder isn't a good professor, I'll try to switch out—"

"It's too late for that," she sniffed. "And English can be a difficult discipline."

Wow. She wasn't done with the put-downs. Incredible.

"In fact, have you considered a physical education major? Or maybe art?"

I was pretty sure phys ed and art majors would not be very happy to know her low opinion of them.

Didn't I already have enough people telling me I couldn't handle college? For Christ's sake, I was twenty-one, three years older than most other freshmen. My late start was solely attributable to not believing I could handle college. But when I finally learned to silence those voices as best I could, I realized that yeah, I was smart enough to do any fucking thing I wanted to.

And since I silenced them *as best I could*, that meant they weren't gone completely. They'd never be gone completely. There was always a nagging little devil sitting on my shoulder, dropping seeds of doubt.

The bastard.

And I didn't need another doubter. I was done with this meeting.

"Thank you, Krishelle," I said just to annoy her. I extended my hand. "I appreciate your help. And *support*."

Her mouth puckered like she'd sucked a lemon, and she reluctantly took my hand, which she shook about as weakly as anyone I'd ever met. Gross. I hated a bad handshake.

I turned on my heel and as soon as I was out of her office, raced down the hall to get the hell out of the building. I hurried around the corner to ensure there was no way I could possibly run into her, and sat down on a little curb.

That's when the hot tears began to drip down my face.

Dammit. I hated crying. I hardly ever did it. But sometimes the universe threw so much shit your way, there was just no stopping the waterworks.

I blew my nose into the bandana stuffed down the side pocket of my backpack. I never felt sorry for myself for long. It was a waste of time if you asked me.

I pushed myself to my feet to head over to the fitness center, where I was due for another thrilling two-hour shift.

"Senna?" a voice called.

I turned. I didn't know anyone at the school yet, so who could have been calling me?

Holy shit.

"Hi, Professor Adler."

11

SENNA

"Well, hello, Miss Duncan. Where you headed?" he asked with a smile that made my knees weak. "Hey, I got your name right, didn't I? I'm still learning everybody's names."

"Yup. Yes. That's me."

Damn him.

I had to get away from him. He'd seen me at Club V, and I was not comfortable with that. No freaking way. I started walking faster. As if that would help.

"Oh, um, I have a part-time job at the fitness center. I have my shift in a few minutes," I said, nearly jogging.

"Oh cool. That's exactly where I'm going right now. It's my day to work out with weights."

Great. Just great.

I forced myself to smile and slowed for him to catch up.

"Hello, Professor Adler," some pretty girl said, passing us.

He nodded.

"How are you liking the university so far?" he asked politely.

I hated small talk. Why couldn't he have just walked by himself?

I looked straight ahead. I didn't need to look at his perfect bone structure marred only by a slightly off nose, messy blond hair, and glasses. I'd seen all I needed to of him the night I'd shaken my ass in his face.

Speaking of which, I wondered if I should just pull the elephant in the room into the open. Tell him I knew he'd seen me, and that I'd appreciate it if he could keep it to himself.

But I didn't have the balls. So I pretended nothing had happened.

"It's great. Yeah, really good," I said.

He didn't need to know any more about me than he already did.

It wasn't that I was ashamed, as such. It was just that I was starting a new life, that of a student, and I wanted to be viewed differently than I ever had been. Was that too much to ask?

So I figured I'd make some small talk right back.

"Professor Adler! Hi!" another pretty girl said.

Jesus. These women were all over him like flies on shit. No wonder he wanted to walk with me. The man needed a bodyguard.

He nodded at his latest admirer.

"How'd you get into teaching?" I asked.

That was possibly the most boring fucking question I'd ever asked anyone, but it was all I had in me at the moment.

"Oh. Well. That's a secret. I'll tell you one, if you tell me one."

Did he really just say that? Was he flirting with me?

"That's okay. I didn't really want to know," I snapped.

Oops.

But I caught myself in time. "Just kidding!"

He was my teacher after all, and did deserve a measure of respect.

But I wasn't sharing any damn secrets.

"I don't have any secrets anyway," I said brightly.

It was only kind of a lie.

"Are you going to answer my question now?" I asked to take the focus off myself.

"Sure. I was an English undergrad major and loved it, so figured I'd go for a Ph.D. And once you have a Ph.D. pretty much the only thing you can do is teach." He shook his head, laughing, and I glanced over at him long enough to see a shock of hair flop down on his forehead. Just as he raked his fingers through it to push it into place, he looked back at me.

Busted.

"Hmmm. Interesting," I said.

Not.

"I do have another secret to share, Senna," he said, leaning a little closer to me.

Oh shit, oh shit, oh shit. Here we go.

This was where he admits to having seen me dance at Club V, but where he also assures me he thinks no less of me and in fact admires my gumption.

Or some bullshit like that.

I'd heard it all before.

I looked up at him, waiting for the condescending little speech I knew was coming.

"My secret is… I hate teaching Freshman English."

What? That was his secret?

I burst out laughing in relief. I couldn't help it.

"Wow. That is definitely something I'd keep secret," I said. "Why are you doing it then?'

He shrugged. "I have to. Everyone in the department is required to teach it once every few semesters. We rotate through it, and this semester is my turn."

The fitness center was now in view. Thank god. Just a couple more minutes.

"Why do you dislike it so much?"

I didn't really want to engage with the guy, but I was sort of curious why an English professor would have a problem teaching an English class.

He took a deep breath. "Most of the freshmen students aren't really into the class. In fact, most of them hate it."

They hated it? I didn't hate it.

He held the door for me as we entered.

"Well. Here's where I need to go check in," I said, pointing toward the office.

We were facing each other now, and his gaze was unnerving. He looked into one of my eyes, and then the other, like he was searching for something.

Maybe he was. But whatever it was, he wasn't going to find it.

"Is my secret safe with you?" he asked with a half-smile.

A devilish half-smile, I might add.

Jesus, I was in trouble. Attracted to a teacher who'd freaking seen me nearly naked? Not a good way to start my college career.

"Um, sure," I stumbled.

Bastard probably knew he'd thrown me off balance. Evidenced by all the pretty girls greeting him as we walked across campus, he was an expert at that sort of thing.

But if he could dish it out, I could dish it back at him.

"I promise. I won't let you down," I said, cocking my head.

A smile spread across his face. "See you in class, Miss Duncan."

I fled to the office to clock in.

Patti looked up from her desk. "Hey, Senna. Working on the schedule. You all right with Monday, Wednesday, and Friday?" she asked.

"Yeah. I am, thank you," I said, looking out the office window to make sure Adler was gone.

Patti followed my gaze. "Are you checking out that hot professor? Every female on campus is in love with him." She sighed.

"Really? No, I wasn't looking at him."

I put my name badge on and hustled to the check-in desk where I started the tedious task of scanning badges and telling people where the locker rooms, basketballs courts, and indoor track were.

"Hey, do you need a bathroom break or anything?" Patti asked just after I'd gotten started. "You're going to be really busy and I won't be able to relieve you for another hour."

The good thing about working noon to two p.m. was that the gym was busy. Like *really* busy. And that meant *I* was busy. My shifts passed quickly.

I was about to tell her I was fine, but something stopped me.

"Um, yeah, let me run to the ladies' room. Be right back."

I'd only looked around the gym once before when Patti had given me a tour. But this time, I headed straight for the weight room.

I couldn't lie. I wanted to see Adler.

And there he was, soaked in all his sweaty beauty. Sure, he was surrounded by younger, equally fit men, but something about him stood out. He moved with a confidence that the average college guy hadn't yet developed, and a maturity that some of them never would.

He had a white gym towel draped around his neck and occasionally wiped the sweat from his eyes. His mid-thigh workout shorts draped over a muscular ass, and his biceps tested the limits of the faded Wellshire T-shirt he wore.

Holy crap.

He set his weights down and grabbed the bottom of his T-shirt, pulling it up to wipe the sweat from his face.

His abdomen was probably the most perfect six-pack I'd ever seen.

And as he did, he turned and looked right at me.

Shit.

I ran back to my post.

12

PROFESSOR CHASE BALDWYN

"*Bonjour.*"

Benno smirked at me from behind his desk in Well-shire's English department, and motioned toward a seat.

"You pronounce that all wrong, you know," I told him, getting comfortable in the creaky wooden chair opposite.

He shrugged. "What can I say, Chase? I teach English, not French."

"And an English teacher you will stay."

I looked around Benno's office. This is what a *full* professor got. It might not look like much at a glance, with its crowded bookshelves, piles of papers, half-dead ivy plant, and one dingy window, but that wasn't the point. To have your own space in a university? It meant you'd *arrived*.

I, on the other hand, as an adjunct teacher, got a shared desk in a windowless room stuffed with a bunch of other academic wanna-bees. It was noisy, smelly, and impossible to get anything done in.

"Hey, I see you've acquired the obligatory Shakespeare poster. Tell me, do they require everyone in the English department to post one of those on their walls?"

He glanced over at it. "It was here when I moved in. I suppose I could replace it. But I'm not much of a decorator. How are things over in the bullpen?"

That was the perfect name for the insufferable 'office' I'd been given to share. "Same old, same old. I spend as little time there as possible. I basically come to campus, teach, and go back home."

Adjuncts didn't have to offer office hours like real professors did. If a student wanted to meet with us, they had to set something up by email and we'd meet in the library, student union, or outside in one of the school's quads. It was one of the many ways the university underscored the hierarchy among its teaching staff and saved money. It was all good though.

Well, it had been good until recently.

"Dude. The language department head came by and

read me the riot act for how I dress." I looked down at my jeans, faded concert T-shirt, and flip-flops.

He had a point.

Benno, by contrast, was wearing standard professor fare with his white button down, khakis, and tweed jacket. All that was missing were telltale elbow patches.

That shit was just not my style.

"He said he didn't want me looking like a student. I don't understand the big deal. I'm not much older than the students, and besides, what does he expect me to do on an adjunct's pay?"

Yeah, I was perpetually broke. Always had been. Probably always would be at the rate I was going.

Benno nodded sympathetically. "It's rough, man. One of the things I don't like about academic life is that they treat full professors like gods and most everyone else like slaves."

He wasn't kidding. The pecking order in universities was legendary. It was amazing that someone like Benno even hung out with me, that's how stratified the system was. But we'd met through the university running club, along with Jamie, which put us on equal footing.

Well, not completely equal. I was a far better runner than he. So I had that.

I rubbed my hand over my face. "Maybe I'm not cut out for university life. I'm just not that good about figuring out the unspoken rules and then following them."

"What else do you want to do?"

Good question.

"I'd love to go back to France and bum around. Get a little bartending job or something like that. Meet a little hottie…"

Benno glanced at his wall clock. "Hey, I have a student coming by in a bit. But I have a thought for you. Jamie's talking about opening a bar."

Jamie? A bar?

"I thought he was happy as a pig in shit teaching his math classes."

Math. Never my strong suit. I was a language guy through and through. I lived for the humanities, even though I knew they would never lead to a decent-paying career. I didn't need much though. I'd grown up in the foster system, never knowing my real parents, so a little stability was all I was really after.

"He does like teaching math. But because of his, you know—family history—the new department head has indicated he'll never be more than an associate profes-sor. He's holding all that shit his father did against him."

Wow. Guess I wasn't the only one with career problems.

"So now he's talking about opening a bar? Does he know how much money that costs?" I asked.

Benno shrugged. "He seems to. But he has the dough, so there are no issues there."

Christ. I knew Jamie had money from his previous

life, but never knew he had *that* kind of money. I couldn't begrudge him, though. He'd been through the wringer with a shit ton of family drama.

Benno started organizing papers on his desk. "We're meeting Jamie later at the fitness center. We can see what he's got in mind. I know he'll be looking for people to work with him, and who can he trust more than you?"

"That's interesting—" I started to say.

But I was interrupted by a knock. It was office hours for Benno, and time for me to hit the road. I stood to leave when he hollered *come in*. When the door opened, however, my feet were glued to the ground.

"Hi, Professor Adler."

"Come on in, Senna. Do you know Professor Baldwyn?" he asked, gesturing toward me.

"I'm not actually a professor yet," I started to say.

But she interrupted me and extended her hand. "Nice to meet you, Professor. Are you in the English department, too?"

Jesus, would that I were. This woman was fucking beautiful with her glossy chin-length black hair. Her sunglasses were pushed up on her forehead, drawing attention to her glittering blue eyes and high cheekbones.

She wore giant hoop earrings and the skinny jeans that were the style of most undergrads, but she was also dressed in some sexy, over the knee high-heeled boots and a leather jacket with fringe. She was more rock 'n roll chick than college chick. And that was fine by me.

Shit. My kryptonite. A hot girl with brains.

Benno cleared his throat to break me of my staring. But if his student was uncomfortable with my male idiocy, she didn't show it.

I cleared my throat. "Um, I teach French. In the foreign languages school," I said, unable to look away.

With her heels, she was almost my height, and a quick and hopefully discreet glance told me she had curves for days.

I think what really got me though, was that she was sexy without trying. Like she was just being herself, and anyone who didn't like it could take a hike.

"Oh. French," she said, politely.

"Ever study a foreign language?" I asked her.

I glanced over at Benno to see if he was ready to boot me. But he just wore a small smile on his face.

He knew I was taken by her. What man wouldn't be?

She looked down for a second as if she were thinking how to answer.

Which struck me as strange. Either you'd studied a language, or you hadn't.

"Well, the high school I went to had Spanish at one point, but they'd gotten rid of it by the time I went there. My school district was pretty broke."

"Well, that's a shame."

She hesitated, then added, "I do need to add one more class, though…"

Damn. Even the shitty schools I'd gone to had French and Spanish. Thank god, too, because languages were the only things I'd ever been good at.

Maybe I could get her to join my course. "Well, think about French 101. My class still has room in it. Seems like a nice enough group."

She nodded, looking between Benno and me. "Cool. I will. I'll discuss it with my advisor."

"Who's your advisor?" Benno asked.

A half-hearted smile spread over Senna's pretty face. "Krishelle Abalone. She's… interesting." She laughed awkwardly.

The name sounded vaguely familiar, but when I looked at Benno, I knew why.

His complexion had gone pale, the pleasant expression erased from his face. "No shit," he said.

Wow. Didn't take him for one to swear in front of students. Unless there was more to the story.

Oh, right. Now I knew why that name was familiar. "Benno, was she the one who—"

But he looked at the clock and cut me off. "Hey, we're running out of time. Let's get down to business, Senna."

Right. My cue to leave.

"Nice meeting you, Senna. Hope to see you in French."

"Thanks. Bye, Professor Baldwyn."

When I closed the door to Benno's stuffy office, I took a deep breath in the deserted hallway.

God, I hope she signed up for my French class.

13

CHASE

JUST A FEW HOURS LATER, BENNO, JAMIE, AND I MET AT the fitness center to start our long-distance run.

"Must be my lucky day. Seeing Benno twice in one eight hour stretch," I said, slapping him on the back.

Jamie scoffed. "I don't call that lucky. Who wants to see that bastard even once in a day?"

Benno cuffed him on the shoulder as we entered the center.

"Guys, did you know Senna works here at the front desk a few days a week?" Benno asked, lowering his voice.

Both Jamie and I whipped around and looked at him.

Okay. I clearly wasn't the only one smitten with the woman.

"Really?" Jamie asked. "Hey, did you tell Chase about her?"

Benno looked around. "I will. But not here. Let's change and then get outside where we can talk."

Once in our running gear, and with a bandana tied around my forehead, the three of us met on the grass outside the fitness center, where we began our pre-run stretches.

"Hey, Chase, you make any progress on your adoption research?" Jamie asked, reaching for his toes.

I stopped, looking up at the blue sky. "Nah. I think I'm going to drop it."

"Really? I thought you'd found your birth parents," he said.

"Yeah, I did. My father is apparently deceased, and my mother didn't want to meet. So it's dead in the water."

Benno stopped his stretching. "Jesus. I'm sorry. That's terrible."

It was terrible. And I didn't want to think about it any more than I already had.

I straightened my legs in front of me and reached for my toes. "Jamie, Benno tells me you're thinking of opening a bar. What's up with that?"

His face brightened. "I am. And believe it or not, I looked at a potential space yesterday."

Jesus. He wasn't wasting any time.

"Hello, Professor Adler," some hot young thing called out.

Jesus, that bastard had more women throwing themselves at him.

He just waved, barely turning his head to see who it was.

Jamie looked at me and laughed. "It's hell being the sexiest professor in the West. Just ask Benno."

"Eh, fuck off, both of you," he said.

"Ben, what are you going to do with all that under-grad pussy being thrown at you? You got some left-overs for Jamie and me?" I laughed.

He scowled at me. He was fun to goad.

"Anyway," Jamie said, "I may have found a space."

"Wow. You're on fire," I said.

He shrugged. "If I don't get my full professorship, and it doesn't look like I will, I need to find something else to do. And I've always wanted to open a bar. Don't ask me why. I know it's crazy."

"Well, if my adjunct position doesn't turn into something permanent, I might just join you," I said.

"That would be awesome, Chase," Jamie said, fist-bumping me.

Benno got to his feet. "C'mon guys. The sooner we get started, the sooner we'll finish."

We both groaned. He was right of course. The worst part of a ten-mile run was right before you started, when you could think of every reason in the world why you shouldn't go, and only one reason why you should.

Because once you started, it actually wasn't that bad.

Once we were off with a slow jog, I looked around to make sure we were alone. "Okay, now. What was up with that gorgeous student of yours, Benno? Christ, I couldn't take my eyes off her."

Jamie and he looked at each other, with Jamie shaking his head.

"I went to Club V with some friends for a birthday last week, and a gorgeous woman did a dance for me."

No. Fucking. Way.

Was he going to say what I thought he was?

"Turned out that beautiful woman was Senna, who is in my English class. And whose favorite book is the same as mine," he said.

"*No shit.*"

The man was besotted by any woman who loved the books he did.

"I have more to add to the story," Jamie said.

Jesus. What more could there be?

"I dragged Benno back to the club so I could see her. He left when she came on, but I held out and finally got a look at her."

Benno and I looked at him while we dodged the slower runners.

"Just like she's in Benno's English class, she's also in my math class."

"She is not," I said, almost tripping over a crack in the sidewalk. "She's in both your classes? Jesus, what are the chances?"

Benno laughed. "Dude, what are you gonna do if she ends up in your French class?"

Fucking marry her, that's what.

14

SENNA

"We are not missing this party. I got a babysitter, dammit."

There was no talking Godiva out of the fraternity party I'd made the mistake of telling her about. Slamming her foot on the gas of her yellow Ford Fiesta, she picked up speed to make a light, as if, should we be one minute late, we'd miss the festivities.

It had been news to me, but patiently explained by my fitness center boss Patti, that college students don't just join a fraternity or sorority. You have to essentially 'try out' by attending what are called 'rush parties.' I had no interest in joining anything of the sort, but Patti had promised a blowout event at the Phi Sigma Delta fraternity and begged me to join her. I'd resisted as long as I could and finally caved, fully with the intention of finding a last-minute reason to cancel.

My next mistake was telling Godiva the story, thinking she'd get a chuckle out of the machinations of 'traditional college life,' just like I did.

Instead, she exploded in excitement, and immediately lined up a sitter to watch her little guy.

Not the way I'd planned for things to go. And now we were looking for a parking spot outside a mansion that looked like something out of *Animal House*. I could just imagine the place full of drunk dumbasses like in the movie, with girls fawning all over the guys while they figured out the fastest and easiest way to get laid.

Sure, there might be some cuties there—Patti had sworn there would be. But I had no expectations and besides had no time for dating, even if the opportunity presented itself.

Christ, my head was still reeling from my office hour appointment with Professor Adler.

I'd met his friend from the French department, Professor Baldwyn, a rockstar-looking guy if ever there was one, with his ponytail, jeans falling off his hips, sleeve tattoo, and leather bracelets. And as if that weren't hot enough, he had crazy-deep dimples when he smiled, and the most perfect lips I'd ever seen on a man.

I kind of wanted to sign up for his French class just to be able to look at him.

Adler had more or less kicked him out of his office when he kept trying to chat me up, and when we got down to business, it turned out he liked my idea for the term paper he'd assigned us on our first day, which he'd give us a couple weeks to write. He probably thought I was sucking up by choosing to write about Somerset Maugham, but the truth was, he really was my favorite author. His stories were so raw, the way they exposed human weakness. Something about that spoke to me. The fact that he was also Adler's favorite had nothing to do with it.

But it was still a cool coincidence. I wasn't used to meeting people who liked Maugham. Or people recommending bookstores to me, even if the proprietor *was* a rude prick.

"Okay. Are you ready?" Godiva giggled, adjusting her boobs.

Oh, for heaven's sake.

"Let's go," I groaned, getting out of the car and heading toward a crowd of people with red cups of beer in their hands.

"Hey, Senna!" a voice hollered over the loud music after we'd done a couple laps through the crowd.

What? I didn't know anyone there but Patti.

I couldn't make out who'd called my name until a gigantic hand landed on my arm. Godiva's eyes widened before I realized it was Ty's hand, the non-reading dunce from my English class who also happened to have a convertible he used to impress girls.

It just figured he'd be here.

"Hi," I said to him, just loud enough to be heard over the music. I didn't want him to think I was excited to see him. "This is my friend, Godiva."

He glanced in her direction briefly, muttering, "Hey," and turned right back to me.

What a dick.

"Great party, huh?" he said, rocking to the music.

Godiva stepped up to his ear. "Where's the beer?" she asked.

He pointed across the room.

"Be right back," she said, and began to weave her way through the crowd, leaving me alone with him.

She probably thought she was doing me a favor. I'd be sure to 'thank' her later.

"So when are we going out, Senna?" Ty asked, his head cocked.

I so wanted to be a bitch to this jerk.

"Um, Ty, I thought I told you we weren't."

Shit. Where was Godiva? Did she get lost?

He stepped closer to me. "C'mon. I know you don't mean it. After all, a girl who works at a strip club ought to say yes when a nice guy asks her out. Most guys wouldn't have anything to do with her."

What. The. Fuck.

Please let me have misheard him, I begged nobody

in particular. I didn't want to knee anyone in the balls so early in the evening.

"Um, what did you say?"

He brushed his fingers across the back of my neck and smirked. "You heard me. A girl like you doesn't have a lot of options, even if you are hot as shit."

There were a multitude of ways to handle something like this, but I chose the nicest I could think of.

I got right in his face.

"I wouldn't go out with you if you paid me."

I must have screamed the last words pretty loudly because everyone in the vicinity turned to face us.

I'd had guys fuck with me before for being a dancer, but I'd always told them to take a hike. I wasn't embarrassed of what I did, although I sure as hell had hoped to keep it quiet at Wellshire.

Undeterred, he put his lips against my ear while pulling my head closer to him. "Do you want everyone here to know you're a stripper?"

"Here's your beer, Senna," Godiva said, returning.

Perfect timing.

"Godiva, Ty here just threatened to tell everyone I work at Club V, after he told me no guy would date a woman who danced there, anyway."

Her pretty eyes turned dark. She was one woman you didn't want to mess with.

She stepped up and got right in his face as I moved out of the way. "You didn't really say that, did you?

Please tell me my friend is kidding. Because I have a knee aimed at your balls right this second."

He took a step back, his eyes widening in horror. "Go fuck yourselves. Both of you. But don't forget about what I said, Senna. Your secret could very easily get out. How'd you feel if Professor Adler knew about your chosen profession?"

"Fuck off, Ty," I said, taking Godiva's arm and leading her through the crowd to find Patti.

He could tell Adler anything he wanted. Wait till he found out our dear English professor already knew.

15

SENNA

I PULLED ON A LONG, PINK WIG AND GLUED ON MY MOST radical false eyelashes. I felt the need to go out and dance as a different version of myself.

Well, that, and I wanted to protect my privacy against any other fuckers who might try and use my dancing against me.

I liked the adult entertainment I provided. I might not have stripped like all the other girls did, but I knew I was still sexy, and I had fun doing it. The vast majority of our customers were wonderful, respectful men, and I'd gotten to know some of the regulars so well that they now remembered my birthday.

It was too bad people had to think less of me

because of how I'd chosen to put myself through college.

They could suck it.

So, I disguised myself not out of shame, but because I had a plan and I wasn't letting anyone get in my way. I'd had enough of people planting thoughts that I was somehow less than.

Like my mother.

I'd called her just that morning. Not because I wanted to speak with her—she wasn't much of a conversationalist, at least not since we'd lost my dad so many years ago.

"How're you doing, Mom?"

She grunted. I pictured her pushing herself up on the sofa, where she'd probably been lying for hours. "Senna?"

Who else would call her 'mom'?

"Yes, Mom. It's me."

She sighed. "How are you?" she asked in a dull voice.

There was no point in trying to make small talk with her, so I got to the meat of why I'd called.

"Mom, do you need any money?"

Yeah, I helped support the one person in my life who'd probably treated me the shittiest. It didn't make much sense. But there it was.

She'd been a normal mom until my dad was murdered. Then she completely and totally lost it, getting worse as the months and years passed, while taking it out on me.

She was the first person who told me I could never handle college. Unfortunately, she wasn't the last.

But that was okay. The naysayers fueled my fire. I wasn't going to let them do anything but.

She perked up at the word 'money,' like she always did. I didn't send her much—it's not like I was loaded, for heaven's sake—but I did feel compelled to help her out of some bizarre familial obligation.

"Yeah. I guess I could use some cash. Hey, you still making a living as a slut? In that club?"

Really?

Who the fuck gets offered money and then proceeds to fling the most vile insults possible to that very person?

My mom, that's who.

"I'll transfer some money into your account, Mom."

"Okay, baby. Thanks." And she hung up.

It was as if she'd already forgotten her ugly words. Or maybe she didn't think they were ugly to begin with.

It had taken me all day to shake that shit off.

It was my turn to get onstage. I'd had the DJ queue up *I Love Rock 'n Roll* by Joan Jett, and asked him to blast it as loud as he could.

It was the best way I could get lost and forget any of the stupid shit swirling around me.

16

SENNA

I decided to give studying in the library a try. It didn't make sense to me why anyone would prefer that over the peace and quiet of their own place, so I wanted to make sure I wasn't missing anything.

It quickly became obvious why the library was a popular hangout. Turned out, for most people, it wasn't about studying.

Sure, there were plenty of people with their noses buried in their books, highlighting, underlining, and taking notes. But the majority seemed to be flitting around, socializing, flirting, and just generally doing anything but studying.

Mystery solved.

So, naturally, I was doing my own looking around, trying to understand this thing called 'college life,' and all its strange customs.

Like, what was the deal with that horrendous fraternity party Godiva and I had been to? It was nothing more than an excuse to drink warm beer and hook up—not that there was anything wrong with that. But it seemed like a silly dance of *will he* or *won't he*, with the majority of women standing around in gaggles, pretending to be enjoying each other's company but really surveying the room to determine which guy was going to hit on them next.

I'd hoped the library would make more sense, but as I accepted the fact that I was not going to get any work done there, I returned my things to my backpack.

That's when I spotted Professor Adler at the checkout desk.

Holy crap. I hesitated for a moment, then decided to say hello. Why not? He'd been super nice in his office and hadn't mentioned a thing about my dancing.

"Hi, Professor," I said, approaching him.

His eyes widened in surprise. What? He didn't think go-go dancers studied in libraries?

"Why, Senna. Hello," he said, the surprise fading and turning into an adorable, dimpled smile.

Then he took his glasses off and damn if he didn't barely look older than most of the students.

Ugh. What was I doing?

"Thank you again for helping me think through my

paper on Maugham. I'm pretty psyched to learn more about him. Sounds like a complicated guy."

"He sure is, Senna," Adler said, stuffing a couple books in his satchel. "Hey, want to go get a coffee? I have hours of work ahead of me and feel like I could nod off right here, right now. I need a pick-me-up."

Holy shit. Coffee? Adler and me?

"Um, sure," I spat out before I could think of a reason to say no.

Ten minutes later, we were sitting on an old, lumpy sofa in a super-cool coffee shop just off campus.

"I shouldn't have coffee this late. It's going to keep me up all night. But what are you gonna do?" He added another sugar to his black brew.

"Why do you drink it then?" I asked, blowing on my boiling hot tea.

He shook his head. "Well, for one, I'm an idiot." He dropped his head back and laughed. "And second, I love the taste. I'm addicted."

We sat in silence, each looking around, avoiding the other's eyes. I had no idea what to say, and no idea why he'd invited me for coffee. We knew nothing about each other and probably had nothing in common. And yet I'd jumped at the chance to join him.

Well, nothing in common except Club V. But I think we were both going to pretend that wasn't hanging between us.

And of course, our favorite author.

"So, Senna, do you have family in the area?" he finally asked.

Grateful for something to talk about, I began to blabber. Because, of course.

Why was I nervous around this guy, dammit? I spent plenty of time around men, both good looking and not so good looking, and it was just business as usual.

But, if I were honest with myself, there was something tantalizing about the student-teacher dynamic. Especially when your teacher was so fucking hot. And had seen you nearly naked. And liked the same books as you.

"No, they're downstate. My dad is deceased, and my mom is… disabled."

That usually put an end to the family talk.

But not with Adler.

"How'd you lose your dad?" he asked, waving at a pretty young coed who had called at him from across the café.

"It's kind of a crazy story. When I was ten, he went over to the neighbors because he heard screaming. Turned out they were having a fight. A domestic disturbance, as the police called it. My dad got shot."

The tragedy of the story always got people, and from the expression on Adler's face, he was no different.

"Jesus Christ. That's awful. I'm so sorry."

Before we could get into how my mom lost her mind after she lost my father, I changed the subject.

"Hey, I visited that bookstore you told me about."

"Thidwick's! Isn't it great?"

Um, no.

"They weren't too… welcoming. Let's put it that way."

He frowned and put down his coffee. "What do you mean?"

I took a deep breath. "I guess I'm not their normal customer. They kind of chased me out when all I wanted to do was browse."

"Are you kidding me?" he said, shaking his head. "God. I'm sorry. I had no idea they were that way."

"That's because you look like the kind of person who belongs there."

He shook his head. "What a bunch of assholes."

He rubbed his chin, clearly trying to make sense of the difference in our experiences there. But before he decided to pity me, I took control. Or tried to.

"Professor, why did you ask me to coffee?"

A huge grin broke out across his face, and his eyes crinkled just the smallest amount. After looking at his coffee for a second, his gaze returned to mine, and he stared. Like he could see inside me.

But I wasn't going to squirm. That was what other girls did.

He took a deep breath. "I like how unapologetic you are."

What the hell did that mean?

He saw the confusion on my face and leaned closer. "Look. We both know I am aware of your work at Club V. And instead of being embarrassed or worse, you hold your head up high. As though, if someone thought less of you, it was their problem instead of yours."

A warm blush washed across my face. Compliments always did that to me. I guess because I wasn't used to them.

"You know how much strength it takes to do that?" he asked.

Holy shit. I didn't think I'd ever had anyone say something like that to me. It was so… kind.

A lump started building in my throat. Time to get the hell out of there.

"Well, I had better get going. I still have a lot of studying to do. I added Professor Baldwyn's French class."

He smiled at that, putting the plastic to-go lid on his coffee.

"Happy to give you a ride to your car," he said.

Looking outside, I realized it was already dark. "Thanks. That would be great."

We rode in silence.

"I'm just up here on the right. The white Honda Civic," I said, pointing.

He pulled up next to my car and stopped, putting his own in *park*.

Oh god. Why did he do that?

My heart pounded. "Thank you for your kind words back there in the coffee shop," I said. "I didn't mean to seem ungrateful. I guess I was just surprised."

"You're welcome," he said quietly.

I grabbed the door handle.

"Wait. Here is my phone number. Text me next time you want to go to Thidwick's. I'll go with you. Teach them a lesson."

I took the scrap of paper from him. Professor Adler had given me his phone number.

Why did I want to jump up and down and scream in delight?

"And don't take too long to text me. Because until you do, I won't have your number."

He wanted my number? He wanted my number!

But wait a minute. Maybe he did this with all the undergrads he could butter up with flattery.

"Thank you. Good night, Professor—"

But before I could jump out of his car, he put his hand on mine.

And then leaned closer until his lips were on mine.

Holy shit. Professor Adler had just kissed me.

17

BENNO

Dammit. After that kiss, all I could think of was the lovely Senna.

And every woman I saw on campus with chin-length black hair looked like her from a distance, too.

I was a fucking idiot. I knew better than to fall for a student.

Sure, over the years, I'd been attracted to any number of beautiful, young women. The university was full of them, and sometimes it was torture, not being able to act on my strongest instincts. While it wasn't against university rules, getting involved with students was advised against. And my personal belief was that it would invite nothing but a shit ton of problems. The balance of power was too out of whack for it to work out well for anyone.

Then why Senna? I barely knew her.

But I did know I admired her.

I put my head down and plowed through the campus's morning crowds, late as usual for my eight a.m. Not only was I not a morning person, but I was shit at being on time.

I looked up as I neared Hobart Hall, and damned if I didn't *really* see Senna this time, just a few yards away from me.

I resisted the urge to jog and catch up to her. Nothing good could come of us becoming involved, or even becoming friends for that matter. I knew I could never keep it platonic. And I kind of hated myself for it.

It was actually interesting, watching Senna make her way across campus toward class, hustling so she herself would get there on time. She wore her usual skinny jeans, accented by some wild-looking red cowboy boots, and had her short hair pulled back into a tiny ponytail. She wove in and out of all the other students rushing to class, minding her own business, lost in thought.

But the other students weren't as lost in thought, particularly the guys she passed on her way.

I spent time around young college men all day, and I knew their biggest weakness was their inability to control themselves around a beautiful woman. The kind of discretion they needed would elude most of them until they got a little older. But I'd never seen heads turn the way I was now, in Senna's direction.

Jesus. They were like fucking dogs in heat.

And being the no-nonsense person I knew her to be, it probably bugged the shit out of her.

As I drew closer, one young man even went as far as to stop her. I couldn't hear what he was saying, but I didn't need to. It was the same thing any ballsy guy said when trying to get to know a pretty girl. And the same thing I would have said at his age.

But when I got closer, close enough to hear the two of them, I could make out that she was turning him down.

Way to go…

And instead of going away graciously, he turned on her.

"Fine. You're not that hot, anyway." He turned on his heel, leaving her dumbfounded at his overreaction, when he turned back to her for one last comment. "Fucking bitch," he said loudly.

Uh-oh.

Dude had just made two serious mistakes. First, he'd called Senna a name. Second, he'd said it in front of me.

As she stood there, her mouth gaping as he walked away, I stepped into his path.

"Excuse me," he said, trying to get around me.

"No," I said firmly.

He looked at me in surprise and tried to step around me again.

And again, I blocked him.

"I heard you. Apologize to that woman," I said.

His head snapped back, and he puffed up to his full size, which was still considerably shorter than I. "Fuck off, man," he said, stepping to the side.

But I moved so I was in front of him again. He wasn't passing until he did as he was told.

"Apologize. You heard me," I said, gripping his arm.

He looked momentarily panicked, obviously not used to being called out, particularly by someone who probably had several pounds on him.

While we were blocking the sidewalk, students streamed past us in every direction, mostly ignoring the encounter. But Senna watched, her eyes wide.

"Do it," I growled.

He looked around. "I'm sorry," he mumbled in her general direction.

"Louder," I said, squeezing his arm tighter. "And look at her."

He looked from me to Senna, and sucked in his breath. "I'm… sorry."

I let go of him with a little push. "Don't talk to a woman like that again, you shithead."

He looked at the two of us, and disappeared into the throng of students.

Senna stood there with her mouth open. She was

astounded. Hell, I was surprised. I had no idea what had come over me. I usually stayed out of student interactions, no matter how ugly or inappropriate they were.

"You didn't have to do that," she said stiffly.

I walked alongside her. "I know."

18

BENNO

SENNA AND I WALKED INTO CLASS TOGETHER, BOTH LATE, which didn't seem to attract the attention of anyone, particularly since the football jerk was right on our heels. He walked into class like he was a star, high-fiving everyone he knew, like they were his subjects.

Dick.

And, of course, because it was just the kind of day I was having, he grabbed the seat right next to Senna.

I started my lecture wishing I could be anywhere else, trying to keep my shit mood in check. I didn't need to take my anger out on the wrong people.

With the exception of Ty, that was.

Senna faced forward in her seat, taking notes, and

referring to the book we were discussing. But Ty, who was not even pretending to pay attention, kept leaning across the aisle to talk to her.

She ignored him, of course. But it was clear he was bothering her. The other students around them tittered, not wanting to tell a star athlete to shut the hell up so they could learn something.

So I decided to do it.

"Ty, can you read to us from the personal essay you brought today?"

Momentary confusion crossed his face, as he clearly had no idea not only what the assignment had been, but also probably didn't even know what a personal essay was.

His bewilderment was replaced by a cocky grin. He sat back in his desk and threw his hands up. "Sorry, Prof. I got nothing."

He looked around, chuckling, proud of his smart-ass answer. Several students followed his lead.

But I was not in the mood.

"Ty, why do you bother coming to class if you're not going to do the work?" I asked.

The room went dead quiet, and Ty's face turned pink then red.

I got him.

He pressed his lips together and said nothing, turning in his seat and facing the front of the classroom.

We worked our way through the class until it was Senna's turn.

"What have you got for us, Senna?" I asked, motioning for her to stand up like I had all the students do when it was their turn to read.

She smiled slightly and pushed herself to her feet. This wasn't an easy assignment, first writing something personal, and then having to share it. But I'd had my students do it since I'd started teaching. It hadn't killed anyone yet.

She cleared her throat and looked around the room. A couple of the guys nudged each other.

Boneheads.

"Um. Okay. Here goes. The Day My Father Was Murdered…" she began.

"My dad was a good guy. An excellent guy, really. The best dad I ever could have hoped for. But I lost him when I was only ten years old."

She hesitated, then took a deep breath.

"We lived next door to some people my mother always referred to as *trashy*. My dad never called them names, but instead recognized that maybe they hadn't had as many opportunities as our little family had. He was always nice to them, even when they were inconsiderate of us.

"One night, when I was in bed, I could hear shouting coming from their house, keeping me awake. Their baby was crying, too. So I went downstairs to where my parents were watching TV and told them.

My dad said he'd have a talk with them. And he never came home."

You could have heard a pin drop in the room as Senna's voice caught momentarily. She finished the story of her father, and there was a brief silence.

While she'd told me her story the night I'd kissed her, I'd never had a student share something like that in class. To hear her do that was to feel that much closer to her tragedy.

I think I respected her even more now.

"Anyone have any comments on Senna's essay? Do you think she covered all the elements that make a strong one?"

I looked around the room, full of the shocked faces of students who'd mostly elected to talk about the trips they'd taken and sports they'd played.

Goddamn, Senna was amazing.

"Okay. Who's next?"

19

BENNO

I SPOTTED JAMIE AND CHASE ACROSS THE ROOM AT THE Faculty Club and made my way over to them, my head down in the hope of avoiding anyone who might want to make small talk.

"Hey, guys. Sorry I'm late." I grabbed the seat facing out into the room. It was the only one available that either wasn't piled high with computer bags, or occupied by one of the guys.

"Why'd we have to meet here? You know I hate this place," I said.

Jamie shrugged. "Put your big-girl panties on. You'll be fine."

Chase said nothing. As an adjunct teacher, he

couldn't enter the club without one of us guys. But I could see he'd dressed for the occasion—more or less—by wearing a collared shirt and his motorcycle boots instead of his usual flip flops.

"Oh, shit," Jamie said under his breath.

I looked up to find Krishelle Abalone approaching our table and steeled myself for something unpleasant.

"Hi, guys," she tried to say breezily. But there was nothing breezy about Krishelle. Everything she did was carefully thought out with purpose and cunning. There was nothing nice or sincere about her. Why she was still with the university baffled me. People saw her coming from a mile away and turned in the other direction to avoid her.

Unfortunately, that evening, there was no escaping her, pinned to our table as we were.

"Benno, I have one of your students as an advisee," she said.

So what? She probably had a lot of my students as her advisees. The university was only so big.

"Um, yeah, I think you're talking about Senna Duncan. She told me when we were discussing her work the other day. She's a smart woman," I added before I'd thought through my words.

But the mistake had been made. A dark shadow passed over Krishelle's face.

Due to her own shortcomings as an academic and general human being, it was well known that she was intensely resentful of other women who were either attractive or had bright futures, both students and faculty alike.

In short, she was a witch.

She made a face like she'd smelled something bad. "Well. I don't know about that. She doesn't really seem like… Wellshire material."

Fucking elitist. And to think she was so snotty when she really had nothing of her own going on.

"What's that supposed to mean?" Jamie asked, arms crossed.

Although we already knew the answer.

"It's clear to me she's not well-prepared for college level courses. I doubt she has the intellect, discipline, or resources to continue. I would be surprised to see her back here next semester."

I wanted to jump across the table and wring her scrawny neck. Which she'd probably like since she'd been finding reasons to show up wherever I was since the day I'd started at the university.

I smiled at her. "Well, it's a good thing, Krishelle, that it's not your job to support her college career, and help her make good decisions about her path."

"Seriously," Jamie said, shaking his head. "Tell me, Krishelle, how many students did you shit on today? Shatter their confidence? Make them feel as useless a human being as you are?"

I could always count on Jamie to take things a bit too far.

She pursed her lips together, and lifted her chin, her

poorly bleached blonde hair crunchy with the over-application of hair mousse. "You know what I'm talking about. Just wait. You'll see what happens to her. And as for you, Jamie," she said, looking down on him, "I… I'm going to report that comment to the provost."

"Go for it, babe," he said as she hurried away.

Chase shook his head. "Damn, Jamie. Don't act like you want a career at the university or anything."

He wrinkled his nose. "Fuck that woman. Why is she even still here? She got caught plagiarizing shit years ago, but they let her have an admin position? They should have booted her when they could."

Jamie was right. Krishelle Abalone had no business at Wellshire University, much less advising students.

"We ought to check in with Senna and make sure that witch hasn't done anything too permanently damaging," Jamie said.

"I'll check in with her," Chase said, laughing. "She just joined my French class."

She had each of us as an instructor now. This was some wild shit.

"Guys. She's amazing. She works really hard. She's up against these kids who've studied languages all their lives and joined French 101 for an easy *A*." he said.

I remained silent. Which was a mistake.

"What, Benno?" Jamie said. "You got something going on with her?" he asked.

I debated how much detail to share. I didn't have anything 'going on with her.' But I sure had kissed her.

"Nope. What about you, Jamie?" I asked.

He looked around the room with one raised eyebrow like he always did when he was thinking. "I'd like to get to know her better. If she's open to it."

I looked at Chase. "Me, too," he said.

And I was *me three*, if I were going to be honest.

Chase beamed. "Go for it. Both of you. I've shared women with friends before. It's awesome. And super hot."

Of course Chase had done something like that before, as free-spirited as he was.

Jamie nodded.

But I almost choked on my calamari.

"Huh? Share? Like, we all date her?" I asked.

Chase leaned back in his chair, holding his hands up like a *stop* sign. "Hey. It's just an option. If you're not cool with it, no problem."

Was I not cool with it? And if so, what was it that bothered me about it—the idea of dating a woman who my friends were also dating?

Who the hell does that?

"I… I guess I could think about it," I said.

"Dude. You have to get rid of that old paradigm where each person has only one partner. That's so dated."

Exactly what I would expect Chase to say.

But Jamie spoke up. "Yup, I've been there. Worked out great, until the woman moved back to France."

"Why'd she leave?" Chase asked.

Jamie pressed his lips together resignedly. "She fell in love with one of us. She didn't want to break the group up. So she split. I wasn't happy about it, but it was her prerogative. You know?"

Chase nodded.

So this 'sharing' business was really a thing. I could deal with that. Or so I hoped.

"I'll tell you what, guys. Let's each get to know her, letting her know we are aware of the others. See what happens," I said, hardly believing what I was saying.

I had a feeling once we did that, none of us would end up with her. But it was a gamble I was willing to take.

20

SENNA

AFTER ADLER'S KISS THE NIGHT WE HAD COFFEE, I couldn't stop thinking about him. It was pissing me off. And what was getting further under my skin was that I needed to stop by his office to turn in a late assignment. I wasn't at all convinced I could resist him if I had to.

Which I guess was part of the reason I went. Truthfully, I didn't *have* to drop off my paper. I'd already emailed it. I *wanted* to drop it off.

And he was probably going to see right through me.

Still didn't stop me, though.

When I arrived, his office door was closed. I could

hear a conversation from the other side, and it included a woman's voice, talking and laughing.

I knocked quietly, both hoping and not hoping I was interrupting something.

The door flew open, and the same beautiful woman I'd seen him with at the gym stood there, looking me up and down.

Really?

"Yes?" she said flatly.

Well.

"I have an appointment with Professor Adler," I said, trying to look past her.

"Senna," Adler said, coming up behind the woman, "come on in. This is Professor Moretti. Her office is just next door to mine," he said, somewhere out in the hallway.

She stepped aside to let me in but was in no hurry to leave. "Okay, Benno," she said casually, "I'll let you get on with it. But hey, Molly and I would love to have you to dinner soon. Bring a date if you want."

She turned to slip past me out the door, looking me up and down again before she did.

Adler closed the door behind her.

"Friendly, isn't she?" I asked.

He chuckled. "Don't mind her. She's like a big sister. Overprotective. And nosy."

So were they an item? Or not?

I took a seat and began to rummage through my backpack. "I saw you two in the gym."

He nodded. "Yeah, she's a big jock. Her wife is one of the coaches here at the university."

Wife? Okay. So not a love interest for Adler.

That was a weight off my shoulders. It shouldn't have been, but it was.

"She sure was giving me the once-over. But a lot of people around here do that."

Seriously. I never suspected academics to be so small minded and judgmental. Thank god they weren't *all* like that.

"I emailed you my paper, but I wanted to give you a hard copy as well, and thank you for coffee the other night."

His jaw twitched and he looked at me for a moment, clearly choosing his words. Good. Maybe I'd gotten under his skin, as well.

He smiled. "I… I enjoyed it. Maybe too much."

What the hell did that mean? Actually, I didn't need to ask.

I looked down at my hands. "I feel the same way."

Awkward.

Time to change the subject. "Why was that woman giving me dirty looks?" I asked, hoping to break the spell.

He took a deep breath and let it out slowly. "Well, Senna, some students at the university are looking for shortcuts to good grades. In place of doing their coursework, if you know what I mean."

"So… was she making that assumption about me?

Because if she were, I'll go give her a piece of my mind." I stood to go.

Adler put his hands up. "Wait. Just hold on. She may have jumped to some conclusions, but that's based on what she's seen. It's based on what we've all seen in the academic world."

Really? Some students were so dumb they had to hook up with their teachers to get by? How'd they even get into the university to begin with?

But I didn't care what the other students did. All I knew was that I didn't have to do that to get by.

"Do you think that describes me?" I asked him.

His mouth fell open. "No. Hell, no. I think that's one of the reasons I like you. You're tackling the work like you were meant for it."

Meant for it. I liked the sound of that.

And I'd take it as a compliment.

"Okay, then. Because if you thought otherwise, I'd be very upset."

He smiled, cocking his head. God, I wanted him to kiss me again.

"Senna, if I thought that, I wouldn't be spending the time with you that I have. I see your desire to learn. I like that about you."

He likes me.

God, the room was hot. I needed to get out, and quick. If I didn't, I might just be throwing myself at Adler, and I didn't see how that could be a good thing.

I stood to leave. "I appreciate your support,

Professor Adler. It means the world. I haven't had anyone believe in me like that—"

I stopped myself. He didn't need to know any more about my particularly sad story than he already did.

"I have to get to math class. I'll see you tomorrow."

He nodded slowly, a half smile making his face more delicious than it already was.

"Well, have fun. And tell Professor Carter I said hello."

I pulled Alder's door closed behind me and hustled over to the math building.

How did he know who I had for math? There were more than a dozen instructors. Lucky guess?

Or was there more to it?

21

SENNA

"Can you take an extra shift tonight?" Zin asked the moment I arrived at the club.

Was she kidding?

"No. Sorry. I have schoolwork to do. And an early day tomorrow."

She scowled. But it wasn't my problem. She needed to hire more reliable people.

"Godiva? You available?"

Godiva turned from the makeup mirror where she was applying glitter to her boobs. "Sorry, Zin. I have to relieve the babysitter."

Sadie came to the rescue. Thank god. I couldn't have dealt with Zin's dirty looks all night. "I can stay,

Zin. But just remember, you owe me," she added with a scoff.

Zin didn't think it was funny, but then she never thought anything was funny.

"Thanks, Sadie," I said after Zin had left. "I just can't pull it off tonight. I have homework and stuff."

She shrugged. "No problem. I could use the extra dough. Hope it's a good night," she added, turning back to her mirror to adjust her platinum blonde wig.

I hoped so, too. The schoolwork was piling up, and I wanted to cut back to two shifts per week. But to do that, I had to make more on the nights that I *did* work.

"How's the crowd looking?" I asked.

Both Sadie and Godiva shrugged. "Haven't had a chance to look yet."

Since I was ready to go, I wandered up to the stage and peeked from behind the curtain. The house was full, with some of the regulars sitting front and center. That could mean good tips. But I knew to never count on anything until I had it in my purse.

I scanned the audience as far as I could see into the dark corners of the club. Way in the back, I could swear I saw someone I'd not seen in there before.

But he was someone I knew.

For fuck's sake. Was that Professor Carter, my math teacher?

I looked around to make sure Zin was nowhere in the vicinity and sneaked out alongside the stage and zipped to the back, as if I were going to the bar for a beverage. When I was sure she wasn't looking, I headed over to Carter.

He looked up at me approvingly.

Yeah, he'd better fucking look at me that way.

"Professor Carter, what are you doing here? I'm not sure I'm comfortable with your presence." I took a furtive look around. Zin would explode if she knew I were talking to a guest this way.

He looked guilty for a moment. And while he was deciding what to say, I looked at the tattoos circling his huge biceps.

Damn.

Then he smiled at me. His dazzling smile. "I didn't mean to stalk you Senna. To be honest, I'd seen you here one time before. I wanted to see you again."

Well. At least he was honest.

"Why do you work here, Senna?" he asked.

Was he really asking me that?

"School is not cheap, you know. I have a work-study job at the fitness center, but that pays next to nothing."

He nodded. "Okay. I'm not saying you should leave this job. I'm sure it's lucrative. But if you ever wanted a position in the math department, I could talk to some people for you."

Um, no.

"Well, thank you. That's a nice offer. But I don't think I'd be such a good fit for the math department."

He stood. "Look, I'll take off. I shouldn't have invaded your privacy like this. I'm sorry."

Okay, at least he apologized. More than I could say for a lot of men.

"I'll see you tomorrow in math, okay?" he said. And just before he turned for the door, he moved closer to me, so close I could smell his shampoo.

His gaze zeroed in on my lips. He placed a hand on my hip, touching my bare skin. I inhaled a sharp intake of air as an electric jolt fired through me. He moved closer and pressed his lips to mine, very softly.

And he tasted so good that I pushed my own mouth back against his, hard. He ran a finger down my cheek in an intimate gesture, and as I thought about how I wanted more, I remembered I was at work in a freaking strip club, wearing a bikini top and Daisy Duke shorts.

Was I fucking crazy?

"Um, I've got to go," I said, backing away. "I'm on in a few minutes."

I turned and ran backstage. I don't know if he left then, or hung around for a while. I was afraid to look in that direction the rest of the night.

Holy crap. Now I'd kissed two of my professors. In what universe was something like that okay? And to top it off, they were friends. Come to think of it, my French professor knew them too. They were the triad of gorgeousness at Wellshire University.

Did Adler and Carter want to have a threesome or

something? What the hell were they up to? I'd never had a ménage, as Sadie called it, but to be honest, I'd fantasized about it plenty. Sadie swore it was the best thing ever.

I put my head in my hands, elbows resting on the dressing room table. I had the room to myself for once, something that seldom happened. And when it did, it never lasted for long.

Just as I started to touch up my makeup, my phone vibrated from a strange number.

"Hello?"

"Senna? It's Ty. Ty from English class."

Shit.

I forced calm into my voice. What did he want?

"How'd you get my number?" I asked.

He laughed. "You're a funny girl, Senna. I know a lot of people. They do things for me."

Um. Okay.

"What do you want, Ty?

Another chuckle. "I have a deal to make with you."

Oh, Jesus Christ.

"What?" I demanded.

"If you write the next paper for Adler's class for me, I won't out you and your lovely little profession. The one where you wear bikinis and short shorts."

Holy shit. Had he been there tonight? Was he out there right now?

"Why don't you go fuck yourself—"

"Senna, Senna, Senna," he clucked. "Such language for a lady—well, scratch that. I guess you're not a lady."

"Drop dead, loser—"

But he cut me off. "Fine. Call me what you want. But if you write my paper *and* agree to one date with me, I'd be willing to call things even."

No way. Things would never be even. He might hang Club V over my head for as long as he could, no matter what I did.

"Think about it, Senna. You don't have to decide right now. But I think it's a fair deal."

We were silent for a moment, myself because I was in such shock and couldn't think of a single thing to say. He wanted me to write his paper? We could both get kicked out of the university for a stunt like that. I couldn't risk it.

"Ty, I can't. I just can't. You don't know how much college means to me. I could lose it all," I pleaded.

"Fine. Totally fine. But I will be going to the school newspaper tomorrow to let them know what one of our students does to pay her tuition…"

Jesus. It was one thing for a couple of my professors to know, and even a few of Ty's idiotic fraternity friends, but the whole university knowing about my dancing? That could make my four years at Wellshire very, very long.

I took a deep breath. I was going to hate myself for this, but survival was all I cared about at that moment.

"Okay, Ty. Okay. What's your paper supposed to be about?"

22

JAMIE

I HAD TO HAND IT TO SENNA.

After our brief encounter at Club V, she came into my math class with her head held high, made eye contact, took notes, and asked questions. My stalking did not deter her, and I was glad.

It was a dick move of me, to show up there to satisfy my lust and curiosity. I'd invaded her privacy. I wasn't proud of it.

But damn if I couldn't stop thinking about her. I knew Benno felt the same, and if Chase didn't yet, he soon would. She was different from the other undergrads we were surrounded with. Hell, she was different from *any* of the women we usually met. Not to mention stunning, with her badass haircut and clothes. She just did not give a fuck, and that thrilled me to no end.

And kept me up at night, rubbing one out.

"Okay, guys. Here's your first quiz. It's brief, and is based on the homework you've been doing, so it shouldn't be too hard."

When I handed the test to Senna, she smiled and said thank you, just like it was any other day.

While the class took the test, I kept a half-assed eye on them to make sure they didn't cheat, scrolling through my email to do some catching up.

Jesus. That pain in the ass reporter from the student newspaper was at it again.

After several requests for interviews, I'd finally met with the kid. He was a senior, but he was small and nerdy, and clearly out to make his name. I knew from my instructor friends in the journalism department that if the students who wrote for the school paper had good stories for their portfolios, they were much more likely to land jobs after graduation. That left the truly ambitious ones to scramble for some good, interesting material that was in short supply on the typical college campus. Seemed they could only showcase so many stories about the school's sports teams, lousy food in the dining hall, and bad plumbing in the dorms.

But *mine* was not a boring story. No, mine offered the promise of drama and dirt, suspicion and betrayal. It wasn't enough that my father was in prison and that

I'd been found innocent of anything to do with his pyramid schemes. There were people who still wanted a piece of me.

I'd thought, when everything went down, that would the end of the whole situation. That it would be put to bed. But in reality, it was just the beginning. And years later, I was still identified by it.

The bullshit my father had heaped on me and so many other people was to follow me for the rest of my life. It was a fact I'd finally accepted, as much as I hated to. And now some ambitious college reporter wanted to use me in his attempt to get a foothold in the after-graduation world.

Gee, thanks, kid.

So I'd finally agreed to meet with him, although there was nothing more to say about how my father had cheated people, and how it had affected the rest of our family and me, which hadn't already been published in the *New York Times*, *Washington Post*, or *Wall Street Journal*. I'd tried to convince the young journalist there was simply nothing new to say, and that anything he needed to know could be had with a simple Google search.

But that wasn't good enough. He was determined to cover the story in the school paper, and if I wanted to have any input, I had to meet with him.

I had to hand it to the little prick. He had some balls.

The issue was that my department head was already

gunning for me and my future at the university. He was convinced I was as crooked as my father and that my association with the university was a black mark against the institution's good name.

Personally, I thought the Wall Street viewpoint I brought to the department was a win-win for everyone, but he didn't see it that way. And I had a feeling this article was going to seal my fate.

So I decided to push a little agenda of my own. If this kid thought he could use me, I'd use him right back, pushing the message that all universities needed more of a private sector perspective, and that's why I'd been recruited to join Wellshire.

"So, Professor Carter, how do you feel about your father's crimes?" was the first question he had for me.

Jesus. If I'd been asked this once, I'd been asked it a hundred times.

"Well, Alex, as you can imagine, it was devastating to my mother and me. It's why I left New York to bring my industry experience to the academic arena."

Not satisfied with my dull answer, he rephrased his question. "When you heard about what your father had done, essentially stealing thousands of people's savings and retirements, what did that do to you?"

He was actually pretty good. Reporters were supposed to dig like he was. But that didn't mean I was going to tell him shit.

"Like I said, Alex," I continued patiently, "it was

devastating. I'm really glad I landed here at Wellshire to leave all that behind."

He looked down at his notes for another question.

"Given your reputation, Professor, do you think you are doing Wellshire any favor by being here?"

Fuck. He'd clearly interviewed my boss before me, who apparently had been pretty generous with his opinions.

But I could handle it. I'd dealt with tougher questions, that was for damn sure. "Well, Alex, only my students can tell you that." I laughed. "Education was always my first love, and I like to think I'm making an impact in my student's lives."

How was that for a can of bullshit?

I'd finally gotten rid of him, tired as he was of my banal answers. But to be honest, the kid never stood a chance. I kind of felt sorry for him. He'd just wasted his time.

But on the other hand, fuck him. He was using my misfortune to showcase his journalism chops.

Not that it had done him much good.

When you'd come through shit like I have, you know how to answer every question and hold your head up in the face of adversity.

I think that was what I liked about Senna. I got the feeling you could knock her down, and she'd somehow manage to pop right back up.

There was rustling in the room as my students were starting to finish their tests.

"Hey, guys, can you please add your email to your tests in case I have any questions for you?" I asked.

One by one, they finished, leaving the room quietly. As soon as the first completed test landed on my desk, I started grading, something that took me only a few minutes. In algebra, I could see the entire process of how a student arrived at their answer, and could immediately identify what they'd done both right and wrong.

I flew through the tests, eager to get them done so I didn't have to take them home. When Senna handed in hers and left the classroom, I pushed it to the top of my pile. I wanted to see how she'd done.

I ended up wishing I'd graded hers last.

She hadn't done too well.

In fact, she'd failed.

Not what I'd expected.

But all was not lost. It gave me an excuse to reach out to her and offer my help. She wasn't going to fail any more tests if I had anything to do with it.

23

JAMIE

"Thanks for coming by, Senna," I said when she arrived during my office hours.

I gave her a minute to take a seat, in part so I could admire her.

"Thank you for offering to help me," she said tentatively.

Was she thinking about how I'd kissed her at the club? Because I sure was.

"I was disappointed you failed your math test. I can't lie."

Shit. I hadn't meant to sound that harsh.

She looked down at her hands, chagrined. "I'm not happy about it, either. But I'm sort of not surprised. I didn't go to the best high school, so I guess I'm not as well prepared as I might be."

I hated to hear that. The quality of public schools varied so much. It just wasn't fair. Some students had great advantages, and others, like Senna, had to scramble to catch up. If they caught up at all.

"Don't worry, Senna. We'll catch you up with some extra work. That is, if you're up for it." I couldn't make her do the work. But if she accepted my help and pulled her weight, she'd be fine.

She bit her bottom lip and nodded. "I'll get this under control with your help. I really appreciate it."

"Senna, do you know how beautiful you are?"

Fuck it. I had to say it.

And she blushed. She goddamn blushed. Now *that* got my motor revving.

Down boy.

I walked around my desk, propping my ass on its corner so I was right in front of her. I put my hand under her chin and tilted her face to mine.

"In many ways, Senna, you remind me of myself."

Her eyes widened. "I do?"

I bent to press my lips to hers for the second time, happy we were out of the confines of last night's club. I wanted to do more exploring with her, if she were on board.

And it seemed she was. She pushed herself to standing and leaned into me, slightly parting her lips.

I put one hand behind her neck and the other on

the small of her back to pull her against me, not caring if she found out about what was now a full-on erection in my pants. Tilting her head, I trailed kisses down the side of her neck, which I'd been dying to touch since the first time I saw her.

She smelled goddamn amazing. No perfume, just clean, sexy girl.

She jumped when someone knocked on my office door.

Jesus. Really? Talk about bad timing.

"Is that your next meeting?" she whispered.

"I don't have anyone coming after you. Let's see who it is," I said, wondering if it was my douchebag department head. I grabbed the school newspaper to cover my telltale excitement.

"Oh. Hey," I said, stepping aside and letting Benno in.

"Hey," he said. But when his gaze landed on Senna, his face lit up in a smile. "Senna. What a nice surprise."

She'd moved a respectable few feet away from me. "Hi, Professor Adler. I was just in here to get some help on pulling my math grade up." She looked nervously from one of us to the other. "I failed the first test."

Benno pushed the door closed behind him and leaned back against it. "Oh, yeah? Math is my weak subject, too. English, I can easily handle, but math is another story."

She shrugged one shoulder. "Guess it's a good thing you teach English and Professor Carter teaches math."

Benno smiled at me knowingly. The bastard. Was he here to cockblock me? Or would we be able to be a bit more creative?

He took a step toward her. "Senna, was Professor Carter just kissing you?"

Oh shit. He was going for it.

Her eyes widened. "Um, yeah," she said quietly.

It wasn't hard to see her mind was racing.

Should I stay?

Should I go?

Should I lie?

Was this going to be a good thing or bad?

He fake-frowned. "Did you tell him I've kissed you, too?"

She shook her head and glanced at me. "Nope."

I bit my tongue to keep from laughing.

"Jamie—I mean Professor Carter—what should we do about Senna, letting both of us kiss her?" Benno said.

"Um, am I in some sort of trouble, here?" she asked, frowning.

"Only if trouble means you have to kiss *me* now. With Professor Carter watching."

Damn. Benno was working it. Didn't know he had it in him.

Again, she looked from one of us to the other, puzzling over our smiles. Benno was having a good time winding her up, but I couldn't let her be uncomfortable for too long.

"Senna, we've talked about you," I said.

"You have?"

"Yeah," Benno said, moving closer. "Jamie and I both like you. And we both want you."

Her brows rose, her mouth open. "You do?" she squeaked.

She might be a badass woman, but we'd thrown her off balance. Which was not a bad thing every now and then.

Fuck, this was going to be fun. I had no idea whether Benno had ever done anything like this, but I sure as hell had. And it had been way too long.

I stuffed my hands in my pockets to keep myself under control. "Kiss her, Benno. I want to see it," I growled, my dick raging harder.

Senna looked my way with a small smile. I nodded. She stepped toward Benno, who tangled his fingers in her short black hair, tilting her lips to his, kissing her sweetly.

C'mon, dude.

But when she put her hands in his own hair and a little moan escaped her, he groaned, parting his lips and pulling her closer.

Then he abruptly let go.

She stumbled back, gasping at the sudden movement and wiping a finger over her lower lip.

Benno looked at her, then nodded in my direction.

Fucking hot.

A sly smile grew on her face. It was easy to see that

the game we were playing had morphed from intimi-dating to something delicious and naughty.

I approached her, not even bothering to hide my erection, and she kissed me with all the passion I'd hoped she would, exploring with her tongue while her breathing deepened.

Benno came up behind her and, while we kissed, removed her velvet blazer to reveal a cropped black T-shirt that pulled tightly across her round breasts, tied in a knot in the back.

Jesus.

I stopped kissing her for a moment to watch his hands touch her exposed abdomen, then wander up to her tits.

"Isn't she beautiful, Jamie?" Benno breathed, pulling her T-shirt up to reveal a black lace bra.

Christ, was there anything about this woman that wasn't drop dead sexy?

As he ran his palms over her erect nipples, her eyes fluttered closed, and she leaned back into him.

I returned my lips to hers and after a moment, whispered in her ear, "You good? Everything okay?"

She opened her eyes slightly, and with a languid nod, said, "Yeah. Oh, yeah."

Well, that was all we needed.

While Benno played with her tits, I undid her belt, brushing my fingers over the warm, firm flesh of her stomach.

Sure, I'd seen quite a bit of her when dancing, but never up close, and never had I touched her soft skin.

As soon as I'd gotten her jeans open, I reached my hand into her panties, finding her bare pussy soaked with excitement. I drew my fingers out to taste her, then dove back in.

"Oh god, Professor Carter—" she started.

"None of that. Call me Jamie," I whispered, working my fingers through her wet folds.

"How's that pussy?" Benno asked.

I was thinking I should probably let him have a turn, but he seemed content kissing her neck and pulling her hard nipples.

"So hot, man, and so tasty. You know how good you taste, baby?" I asked her.

She laughed lightly and pushed harder onto my hand.

Taking the hint, I shimmied her jeans down just below her thighs and slipped a finger inside her tight walls.

She gasped. "Oh god. Like that."

So I slipped one more finger inside and began pumping her pussy, the heel of my hand pulsing against her clit.

"Fuck her, man," Benno growled. "Make our beautiful girl come."

"Oh, oh, oh," she moaned, her breath raspy. Her head bucked back and forth, and she ground harder against me.

Her orgasm hit like a freight train, and it was all Benno and I could do to hold her up.

It was one of the hottest fucking things I'd ever seen.

"Oh my god," she said after a few moments, shaking her head. "Holy shit."

Holy shit was right.

"Professor Adler, Professor Carter, " she said after she'd caught her breath. "I think now it's time to try something new."

24

SENNA

I DIDN'T KNOW WHAT I WAS DOING, AND I WASN'T GOING to stop long enough to think about it.

Fuck thinking. I'd been doing enough of that. I wanted to *feel*.

And in particular, feel two of the hottest freaking professors the universe had ever known. Yeah, I figured what we were doing was unethical on some level. But we were consenting adults, and I figured as long as we were honest about it, no one would be hurt.

And I was too damn turned on to stop and think any further about things.

With my jeans below my ass and my shirt and bra pushed up above my boobs, I looked from Adler to

Carter, wanting to pinch myself at my great luck. The ball was in my court, and I was pretty sure I knew what to do with it.

I kicked off my boots and pushed down my jeans far enough to step out of them, and lifted my bra and T-shirt over my head. Then, I lowered myself to the chair I'd been sitting in for my meeting and reached for Adler's belt and fly. Through a tangle of shirttails and boxers, I found his enormous hard on and pulled it out. I turned to Carter and did the same thing.

I now had a cock in each hand and slowly began to run my fingers over each from the top down to the balls. Carter's eyes fell closed, and he pushed into my grip, while Adler watched my every movement.

Oh my god. I was doing it.

"Such nice cocks," I murmured.

They both smiled.

"I think I'm going to taste them."

They smiled bigger.

First, I took Adler into my mouth. His precum was salty and delicious, and when I took him to the back of my throat, he was so long, I worked the length I couldn't fit with my hand.

"Fuck, baby," he groaned. "You almost took the whole fucking thing," he groaned.

I turned to Carter. His cock, by comparison, was not as long but was fatter, so fat I had to stretch my mouth to its limits to take as much of him as I could. His shaft was smooth and soft against my hungry lips.

I went back and forth, from Adler's cock to Carter's, taking turns sucking one and jerking the other, then the other way around.

I didn't want anyone to feel left out.

"Stand up, baby," Jamie said authoritatively, bending me over the edge of his desk. "And keep sucking Benno."

Oh my god.

I took as much of Benno as I could while Carter, behind me, opened his belt and pants.

He ran his finger through my slit, spreading my moisture, and caressing my ass cheeks. Then he leaned next to my ear.

"I'd like to fuck you, baby," he said.

I almost exploded right there.

Pulling Adler out of my mouth, I whispered, "Do it."

I heard the ripping of a condom wrapper and the rolling sound of Carter sheathing himself. His cock ran up and down my puffy folds and began to push its way inside.

He leaned over me, next to my ear. "Are you ready, baby?"

"Mmmm," I grunted, my mouth full. But if there was any doubt about my intent, I pushed my hips back to make them clear. Jamie's fingers had been nice, but I now needed his dick. Badly.

He pushed inside a couple inches and held himself there, thank god. He was so wide I needed a moment to adjust and let the initial burn fade. When it did, I pulled Adler out of my mouth.

"More. Please."

That was all Carter needed. He plunged into me so hard and deep I screeched before I had gotten back to sucking Adler. Now I had both holes filled. And I fucking loved it.

So hot. So dirty. So naughty.

So *educational.*

Okay, maybe not.

Carter, gripping my hips, banged me like he wanted to own my pussy, which pushed me into Adler, who was holding my head and directing my mouth on and off his dick.

"Fuuuuck," Alder growled, pulling me down on his cock. Reaching the back of my throat, he grew longer still, flooding my mouth with cum. He shuddered and groaned, thrusting again before pulling out and catching his breath. I tried to swallow all he had to give, but some ran down my chin and onto the papers on Carter's desk below me.

Someone was going to get their math test back with a little 'spot' on it.

Pressing my sweaty face onto Carter's desk, I gripped the sides of it for purchase while he pounded me from behind. Another orgasm built, spreading from my core to the ends of my limbs. I was trying to keep it quiet since I was, after all, in one of my professor's offices. But a girl can only be so discreet when being pummeled by a big, fat dick like Carter's.

Behind me, he groaned, driving deep and holding himself there while his cock swelled and throbbed with what I knew was an explosive orgasm. That set off my own again, and I squirmed under him, pounding my fist on the desk underneath me.

When I'd caught my breath, I lifted my head. Through a tangle of my hair and slightly blurry vision, I saw Adler sitting in my chair, watching us both with a massive smile on his face.

25

SENNA

"Girl, you won't believe what I did."

Godiva rested an elbow on Club V's bar, where we'd grabbed seats after closing time. "What?"

I looked around to check for privacy. The coast was clear.

But I leaned closer to her, anyway. "I had a threesome."

Her mouth dropped open, and she slapped my arm. I knew it was meant to be an affectionate swipe, but in her excitement, she'd actually really hit me.

"Jesus. Didn't know you were such a bruiser," I said, rubbing myself.

She ignored my complaint, not about to let

anything get in the way of sex talk. "Shut. The. Fuck. Up."

I looked around Club V, all the customers having gone home. The house lights were turned up bright, and a cleaning crew swept through making the place spotless for the next day.

It really was quite miraculous, what they did. Sometimes, after a busy night, the place was just trashed.

"And guess what else?" I asked.

"There's more?"

I nodded. "Yup. The guys were two of my professors."

Her eyes bugged out of her head, and she was shocked into silence. First time I'd ever seen that.

"Wh… what? How? Where?" was all she could manage.

"I was in my math teacher's office, and the other one happened by. They're friends, as it turns out. And fucking hot."

Jesus. I'd been thinking about it all day.

"Wow. Just wow. I'm so psyched for you. That's hot as shit. Oh my god. My little Senna."

We looked at each other, and then burst out laughing.

"My little Senna? What the hell is that shit?" I asked.

She finished the last of her beer. Neither of us drank much, but she wasn't working the next day, so she'd be okay.

Gotta keep the tummy flat and all that.

"I have no idea. I just didn't know what else to say," she giggled.

It was so nice to relax after a busy night. And it had been a good one for me. Really good.

I'd been so wound up by my session with Adler and Carter, that when I set foot on the stage, it was like I was possessed. I'd never danced with such sensuality. During my fifteen-minute sets, I owned the goddamn club.

And my enthusiasm paid off in spades. The customers I danced for tipped me generously, thanking me profusely for putting on such a good show. It was *the* perfect night until I saw Ty in the back.

Yup, Ty.

At least I thought I saw him. I inched my way in his direction, fully intending to verify whether or not it was him, when whoever it was saw me coming and made for the door.

What a wimp. He had to run off rather than speak to me?

But I didn't let it bother me. I couldn't. I was on top of the world, and nothing was taking that away.

26

SENNA

Back to work the next day at the fitness center, I continued scanning the ID cards of everyone passing through its doors. It was such a menial task that I couldn't help but wonder why they didn't invest in some sort of equipment that would let people badge themselves in. You know, automate the process.

But hey, if they did that, I'd be out of a job. So I kept my thoughts to myself.

"Senna. How are you?"

I looked up to find my French teacher peering down at me. And I mean peering. The man was gigantically tall.

"Oh. Professor Baldwyn. Nice to see you. Are ya here to work out?"

Shit. Did I really just ask that?

Idiot.

But he just laughed, pulling a ponytail holder off his wrist and scraping his hair into it. "Yup. They have a yoga class I've been wanting to try. Hey, do you get off work soon? You could join me."

Oh my god. What a sweetheart.

Was this the *third* professor I was going to end up crushing on?

I looked at my watch. "I can't. I have one more hour of work."

He slung his backpack over his shoulder. "Oh. Perfect. Yoga is only one hour. How about we meet back here and talk about class? I'd chat now, but I'm about to be late."

Then he looked past me and waved at someone.

I turned to see Adler and Carter coming into the gym as they looked from Baldwyn to me, and back.

Oh my god oh my god.

A burning heat washed over my face, certain evidence that I was turning beet red. The very two men I couldn't stop thinking about were heading right for me.

My first threesome.

"Chase. What's up, man?" Carter asked as he and Adler high-fived Baldwyn.

Um, was this some sort of joke?

They'd all arrived at the gym at the same time, just when I happened to be working?

"Senna, nice to see you," Adler said with a panty-melting smile.

Carter winked at me as he handed me his ID card.

They were trying to play it cool, but there was something different in their eyes now that we were a little more than just student and teacher.

Not sure if that was a good thing or bad. But I did know I was about to crawl out of my skin.

But first rub up against them.

"I see you've met Professor Baldwyn," Carter said, gesturing to his friend.

"Hey, I'm not a real professor, you know," he interrupted.

Carter patted him on the back. "Relax, I'm just having a little fun."

Glad they were having fun because I wanted to die.

"I'm in his French 101 class," I squeaked.

Baldwyn's face lit up in a huge smile. "Wow, we're all acquainted. That's awesome. Hey, I gotta run to yoga. Senna, see you in an hour," he said, taking off.

That left me with Adler and Carter, whose eyebrows were raised.

Please, God, could we have an earthquake and could you swallow me up in it? Now?

Adler discreetly squeezed my hand. "How're you doing, sweetie?"

He and Carter looked at me.

I nodded. "Good," I said, flatly.

Oh, what the fuck. What was the use in being coy?

I took a deep breath and shimmied my shoulders to release the tension. I looked around to make sure no one was in hearing proximity. "That was… so much fun yesterday. I'd never done that."

The guys looked at each other with satisfied smiles.

Carter lowered his voice. "Never done a threesome?"

I shook my head. "No. But I might like to try another."

Adler tilted his head. "That can be arranged." He shifted in his trousers.

"Hello, Professors. Is everything okay?" Patti chirped loudly as she approached us.

I spoke up first. "Everything's fine, Patti. We were just discussing class."

Her eyebrows rose. "Oh. You have both these men as teachers?"

Sure do, sweetie.

"Hey, we have a racquetball court reservation we need to get to," Carter said. "See you later, Senna."

"See you," I said, turning back to my boss.

She wistfully watched them disappear into the men's locker room. "God, they are beautiful." She wandered back to her office, shaking her head.

Good lord. What was I getting myself into?

Things slowed as the end of lunch hour drew near. I pulled out my laptop. I'd started that asshole Ty's paper a few days earlier and wanted to finish it to get him out of my thoughts. His assignment had been to write a brief biography about someone famous.

Our conversation about it had baffled me.

"Who do you want to do a biography on?" I'd asked him when he'd cornered me in the hall after class.

"Don't know. Don't care. You choose." He started walking away.

He was a bigger idiot than I'd thought.

He stopped and turned. "Wait. The paper can be about anyone I want?"

Now the wheels were turning.

I nodded.

"Okay then. Do my paper on Kanye."

I didn't think that was the sort of famous person Professor Adler had in mind, but I didn't care about Ty's paper. Only my own.

"Ty, why are you even here, at the university?" I asked.

I had to ask, no matter how bitchy it sounded.

"It's the best way to get into the pros, little lady," he said, wandering off with a wave.

Well.

That left me a lot of options. I decided to write a biography not about Kanye, but about the sort of star that would embarrass the shit out of him.

Taylor Swift.

No meat-loving dumb jock ever liked Taylor Swift. Or at least, no one who'd ever admit to it.

But he was about to become a fan. A big fucking fan.

While I counted down the minutes until my meeting with Baldwyn, I put the finishing touches on Ty's paper, making it just crappy enough to first, look like he'd written it, and second, get him a solid C- on it —if Adler were feeling generous.

27

CHASE

I'D HAD A PRETTY GOOD YOGA CLASS, BUT DAMN IF I couldn't stop thinking about Senna the whole time. And the way she'd blushed when the other guys came into the fitness center just about set me on fire. They'd been together, one way or the other. It was written all over their faces.

And I was cool with that. I wasn't a possessive guy.

But I'd have been lying if I didn't admit that I hoped Senna would be down with spending some time with me, as well.

Or maybe all three of us guys?

"Hey, you off work yet?" I asked when I found Senna still at the front desk.

She slammed her laptop shut.

What was that all about?

"Um, yes. Yes, I am." She waved someone over.

"Patti, I need to head out. Who's replacing me?" she asked.

Patti, who must have been the boss, looked me up and down with a smile. "Oh, go ahead, Senna," she said, practically melting over the counter. "I'll cover for you until Jaden arrives."

Senna looked surprised. "Oh. Okay. Well, thanks." She stuffed her laptop into her bag, and we headed out.

The afternoon sun was blinding, and the temperature was perfect. Small groups of students were camped out all over the campus's perfectly manicured lawns.

This was what I loved about university life. The mellow socializing, talking about classes, sharing, learning.

Not the crap the administrators rained down on our heads. Took nearly all the joy out of it.

But I wasn't going to let it ruin my day today. I had the beautiful Senna right next to me, and I was going to get to know her better.

She might not know that yet, but it was okay.

"Hey, Senna, let's catch a little shade over here," I said, leading her onto the grass next to a tree.

She sat opposite me and crossed her legs. "How was yoga?"

"Pretty good. Pretty good," I said, nodding.

Nothing like what I'd experienced in India, but I wasn't going to let her know I was a yoga snob.

"Ever practiced yoga?" I asked.

"No. But I'd like to."

I couldn't lie. I loved a yoga chick.

She leaned back on her elbows, turning her face to the sun, which brightened her smooth skin. She let her eyes fall closed, which was fine with me. That way I could stare without being a fucking creep.

"So tell me, Senna," I started. "How's French class going for you? I know it's a lot of work—memorization and that sort of thing when you're just starting out. It can be kind of overwhelming."

Her eyes popped open. "That's the perfect word. Overwhelming. I guess I'm not sure where to start."

Of course, I was happy to offer any direction I could.

And more…

"Okay. First, we have vocabulary. You should get some index cards and put the French word on one side and the English translation on the other. Quiz yourself every time you have a few spare moments."

She nodded. "Oh, I like that idea."

"Just keep going over them. Eventually, you won't even have to think about the words. They'll be embedded in your brain. Do the same with the verbs we're learning."

I droned on about language learning best practices

while Senna wrote down a few notes. I had to hand it to her. She was motivated.

"It seems like a lot of the other students have studied languages before."

She was right.

"Yup. By the time most people get to college, they've taken some Spanish or French. It's really hard to be a first timer at the college level. The pace is intense. But I've seen it done before. You'll be fine if you stick with it. And let me know when you need help."

She sat back up, squinting from the bright sun. "Thank you. I appreciate the suggestions. How'd you get interested in French?"

In a convoluted manner, just like everything in my life happened.

"I grew up in foster care but managed to get my undergrad degree—against all odds. After college, I didn't know what else to do, so I joined the Peace Corps. I was sent to the Democratic Republic of Congo and got to learn French. When I came back, there were a lot of graduate school programs giving financial aid to former Corps volunteers, so I stuck with it."

Her eyes widened. "Wow. You were in Africa."

I nodded. Those were crazy days, doing good volunteer work while dodging dangerous characters and diseases like malaria. But I'd made it through unscathed. I was glad I'd done it. Proud, even. But once was enough. Even for a minimalist like me, that level of roughing it was bearable for only so long.

I leaned back on the grass, enjoying the sun baking my skin. But I couldn't lie there all day, and I was sure Senna couldn't either. Even though I would have loved to.

I had to get cleaned up and meet the guys at the faculty club.

I popped to my feet and extended a hand to help Senna up.

When she was standing again, I took a little too long to let her hand go. "See you in class tomorrow?" I asked.

She smiled shyly. A beautiful woman who was modest. Wow.

"Yes. See you tomorrow," she said, and was off.

I watched her weave through the crowd of students until she disappeared out of sight. I headed in the opposite direction, back toward my shared office where I'd stored some clothes suitable for hanging out with the real professors.

28

CHASE

"Mr. Baldwyn. May I see you in my office?"

Everyone in the bullpen I shared with adjuncts like myself turned to see who'd beckoned me.

Shit. Just as I'd feared. It was the head of the French department. This could mean very good news or very bad news. It was unlikely to be anything in between.

I grabbed the clothes I'd come for and followed her to her office, steeling myself for the worst.

"Have a seat, please," she said.

I was already sitting. Guess I should have waited. I still sucked at academic protocol. Actually I sucked at pretty much all protocol. When you grew up bouncing around from one foster home to another, you didn't learn a lot about life's pleasantries.

"Mr. Baldwyn, I'm afraid we won't be able to keep you for next semester—"

My stomach dropped, the warm feeling from just having hung out with Senna quickly disappearing.

Fuck. I knew it. These universities and their budget woes. Fortunately, I'd been thinking about my next move, and Jamie seemed like he was serious about opening a bar, so I didn't need to jump into panic mode. Yet.

"I see," I said calmly.

"However," she said, "if you think you can finish that translation you've been working on for me, we might be able to work something out."

Huh? Was she extorting me?

How was it that the head of a major university's French program had such a lousy knowledge of the very language she was supposed to teach? It blew my mind. And yet she got to stick around the place, thanks to tenure. Well, that and coercing adjunct teachers to do the hard work of writing for her.

I'd heard that back when the school was establishing a French program, she'd come on board first, before anyone knew she was about as unqualified as they came. She'd squeaked by for years, undiscovered. Shit, the university administration probably still didn't know she couldn't write in French. The truth was, she'd write in English and get some poor sap to translate it. And none of the folks who ran the school knew any better. She'd somehow gotten everyone to keep their mouths shut.

By offering them jobs. Real jobs.

"Oh, hey, I'm about halfway done with that," I lied.

It was a boring slog, translating her crappy publication about some obscure mayor during the French revolution. Did she really think anyone would ever be interested in that?

That was the problem with academics. You were pressured to write about obscure topics that no one really cared about, just for the exercise. Just to say you'd done it. Paid your dues.

It was how the game was played, apparently. And I was getting my first taste of it.

"When do you need it, Professor Miller?" Every other professor I'd met at the university went by their first name among other instructors. But the first time I called this one 'Rebecca,' it was like I'd called her the C-word.

She broke out in a smile, smug in the satisfaction that she was pulling another one over on the school. "End of the month?" she cooed.

She could go fuck herself.

But I smiled. "Sounds good. It will be in your hands by then. Or in your email."

She laughed gleefully, satisfied she'd fooled everyone around her for another day.

"CHASE, I saw you looking at Senna today in the fitness center," Jamie teased. "She's something, isn't she?"

I sat back in my chair, surveying the faculty club crowd, which was mostly a bunch of old farts overly impressed with themselves. The younger academics were out spending time with students, trying to make a difference.

But I didn't mind going once in a while. I got a kick out of it. I supposed it was old hat for someone like Jamie, though, who'd grown up with money and apparently still had plenty.

I looked around the room for Benno. He was always late. Always.

"Did you get to hang with Senna after she got off work?" Jamie asked.

I nodded as I sucked down my second beer. "Yeah. She's adjusting to her first foreign language class. It helps if you know how to approach it. Gave her some study practices."

"Uh, yeah," Jamie said. "I barely made it through high school Spanish. My parents actually had to hire me a tutor."

"It's not for everyone. I, on the other hand, barely squeaked by algebra."

We just looked at each other. It was clear he had something to say.

"What is it, dude? Just come out with it," I insisted.

I wasn't into beating around the bush.

"Benno and I are kind of seeing Senna."

I knew it. And I thought it was great.

But I hoped Jamie's 'announcement' didn't mean my chance to get to know her better was off the table.

Because I had every intention of doing so.

"That's cool. Good for you guys," I said as Benno arrived.

"Good for us? What's good for us?" he asked, taking off what I called his 'professor jacket.'

"Jamie was telling me you two have something going on with Senna. That's hot. I hope you guys have left room for me."

Benno laughed. "Oh, we have. Don't worry. We have."

29

CHASE

Next day in class, I was ecstatic to see Senna not only getting the answers right as I went around the room with our vocabulary drills, but also leaning over to help the girl next to her when she got stuck.

Yup, I'd known that with a little push in the right direction, she'd master the course material. In fact, perhaps with even more help, she'd learn to love French like I did.

As everyone was streaming out at the fifty-minute mark, I hollered some last-minute instructions.

"Okay, guys, don't forget to log into the language lab over the weekend. You need the practice." They fled the classroom like their asses were on fire.

Everyone except for Senna, that was.

"Hi, Professor Baldwyn," she said, holding her books in front of her like she was playing hot schoolgirl.

And she'd called me professor. I knew I should correct her, but being called professor had a nice ring. And it might be the closest I'd ever get to being called one, anyway.

"That was fun, going around the room and having to think on your feet," she said, bouncing on her own feet.

But I was imagining her bouncing around Club V.

"Glad you liked it. Nobody really enjoys being put on the spot, but it does get the circulation going."

Kind of like the circulation running to my dick right now.

"Hey, I wanted to tell you something," I said.

Concern crossed her face. "Okay. Is it something with my grade?"

"No, no, no. It's actually more… personal."

She might not like what I had to say, but I was all about honesty. Some people appreciated that about me. Others did not.

"Okay," she said slowly.

I pushed the classroom door closed and walked over to my desk, which she was leaning against.

"Couple things," I started. "First, I know you're a dancer at Club V."

She took a deep breath, waiting for my reaction.

"Hey. There's nothing to be embarrassed about. It's probably helping you pay your way through this expensive school. "

She looked back up. "It is. I have that work-study job in the gym, but it's really a waste of my time. I barely get paid anything. But it's a requirement of my tuition waiver."

I remembered those days. I'd been there, scraping and crafting how to pay for college. It was a bear, trying to figure out how to finance something so important when you had no resources, and no record to prove you were a good investment.

"Was there anything else?" she asked.

Brave girl. She didn't run away from shit.

"Yeah. The professors—shit, can I just call them Benno and Jamie?"

She laughed and nodded.

"The guys told me you are more or less seeing them. We're all friends, and I wanted you to know I knew."

She sucked in her breath. "You're not going to tell my advisor, are you? Or anybody else?"

"Of course not. Fuck those nosy bodies. It's none of their goddamn business."

While her cheeks were slightly pink, she smiled with relief. Fucking beautiful.

"And..." I continued, "I wanted to say I'm interested in you, too."

I walked my fingers across the desk to where hers

were resting and brushed them lightly to gauge her reaction.

She might be receptive. Or she might tell me to go packing.

But she turned her hand palm up so I could interlace mine with her fingers. I lifted her hand to my lips and kissed it lightly.

Her pupils dilated. I pulled her closer and wrapped my free hand around her waist.

This time, kissing her lips.

30

SENNA

Holy shit.

I was kissing my French professor. Or whatever he was.

And I'd just been with my English and math professors.

I'd known college was going to be different, but I sure as hell hadn't anticipated anything like this.

Chase's mouth explored mine slowly at first, and after a small groan, he ground into me with a fury I knew would leave me sore later.

I parted my lips to welcome his taste, and he moved closer, propping me on the desk behind us and wedging himself between my legs.

"Damn, Senna. I had a boner for you the whole fucking class," he said, running his lips down my neck. He slipped my T-shirt off one shoulder, his lips traveling there, too.

Oh my god, this gorgeous, free-spirited man liked and wanted me. He knew my deepest secrets and thought no less of me for them. In fact, I think he liked me even more when he found them out.

He ran his hands through my hair and down my back until he reached my ass. He took handfuls of me, scooting me to the edge of the desk until his hard cock pressed against the seam of my blue jeans. It wasn't the most comfortable sensation, but something about it was primal, like we were desperate for it no matter the discomfort. If we hadn't been in a classroom with an unlocked door, I had a feeling in a matter of moments our skin would be touching rather than our clothes.

And that would have been okay with me.

Jesus, what was I doing?

A little voice was nagging me, saying get your shit together and get out of here. You had no business kissing your French teacher, and he had no business kissing you. But a much louder voice screamed *go for it, girl,* and to relish the experience of being with a man who adores and appreciates you.

I reached behind his neck and yanked on the elastic holding his ponytail, his thick, curly hair tumbling into my fingers. I pulled fistfuls of it close to inhale his scent, which was simple soap and shampoo.

He'd had some raw deals in his life just like I had. Maybe that was what drew us to each other—we shared the ability to see each other's pain, and instead of trying to make it go away, we could help each other walk through it. We'd both been through things we'd never forget. But we knew they didn't need to define us.

Running my fingers along his sleeve tattoo, I sighed into his mouth as his hands reached beneath my T-shirt for my breasts. He maneuvered under my bra and alternatively pinched and soothed my hard nipples. The sensation shot straight through to my core, and I whimpered, aching with need.

Just then, the classroom door flew open, and a young woman stood staring at us like she'd seen a ghost.

"Oh. Oh, sorry," she said, as she began to back out the door.

"No, wait," Chase called. "We're leaving. The room is all yours."

The look on her face, of pure astonishment at finding two people all over each other in what should have been an empty classroom, struck me as hilarious. I pulled myself together and grabbed my backpack, running for the door with Chase right on my heels. As soon as I'd gotten into the hallway, I began to howl with laughter.

Chase shook his head at my reaction.

We just looked like two horny students, unable to wait until we got home.

"Let's get out of here," he said, taking my hand.

We started running down the hall like two maniacs, dodging everybody else, and laughing at the strange looks we were getting.

I COULD HAVE KEPT KISSING Chase all day and into the night if I hadn't had a date with the horrendous Ty. Hopefully, this was my last obligation in his deal to keep his mouth shut about my off-campus job. But I knew better than to trust the bastard and wouldn't put it past him to make some other unreasonable demand, preying on my desire for a normal college experience.

Although, it seemed like my college experience was starting off as anything but normal.

I wasn't complaining.

"Hey, Ty," I said flatly when I met him outside the entrance to the school's basketball stadium. I wasn't about to let him pick me up and find out where I lived.

"Well, if it isn't the luscious Senna Duncan, every teacher's pet," he crooned.

Shit. What else did he know about me?

He tried to swing an arm around my shoulder as we waited in line, but I dodged him, stuffing my hands in my pockets and using my elbows as defense. As long as

I had them pointing out, he could only get so close to me.

He looked through the crowd like he was a freaking superstar waiting for his accolades. And it took only a moment to realize he sort of was, as evidenced by all the greetings and high-fives that came his way.

It was incredible. As we moved through the stadium concourse, packed with people buying hotdogs and Cokes and hurrying so they wouldn't miss the start of the exhibition basketball game, the crowd actually parted for him. He made eye contact with everyone he could, nodding and smiling.

What a narcissist. He was like a politician running for office.

I wanted to barf.

We showed our seat numbers to an usher, whose eyes widened when he saw Ty.

"Come right this way," he said, gesturing that we follow him.

We started down the steep stadium stairs past the *okay seats*, then the *good seats*, then the *great seats*, until we reached the actual floor the game was played on.

I supposed those were the *fucking awesome seats*.

Because, of course. He was a star athlete, and everywhere he went, the red carpet was rolled out for him. No wonder he was shocked I turned down his dates. People like Ty were walking currency, which opened doors closed to us mere mortals.

We took our floor seats, and Ty waved to someone who arrived with a box of snack items to choose from.

"Want some popcorn? Or something to drink?" he offered.

I examined the offerings. "Sure, popcorn. And a water."

The happy servant produced our order and took off as fast as he'd arrived.

"Don't we have to pay him?" I asked.

He looked at me with a proud smile and took a chug of his soda. "Nope," he said, wiping his mouth with the back of his hand.

Jesus.

"I turned your paper in. I mean *my* paper," he said, nudging me.

If Adler—I meant Benno—ever found out I'd written that paper, well, I didn't know what he'd do. But I *was* confident he'd be majorly pissed.

"Cool," I said, looking everywhere but at Ty.

I wanted to make it clear to him that I was there only under duress. He might have thought he could dazzle me with good seats and VIP treatment at a college game, but that shit meant nothing to me. It was a shame such privileges were wasted on such an ungrateful imbecile.

SENNA

THE GAME STARTED AND I WAS BORED FIVE MINUTES IN. I could appreciate that these college athletes were talented and were providing valuable entertainment to fans of the game, but I could give a shit about basketball, and was massively resentful I'd been manipulated into spending a free evening there with a man I was coming to detest.

When the crowd roared over something one of the players had done, Ty leaned toward my ear. "I hope you're having fun Senna, because we are going to do this again."

My head snapped in his direction. I wanted to punch him in his smug face, but I limited myself to glaring. "You're fucking kidding. There will be no more of us"—I gestured between the two of us for emphasis—"after tonight. I'm only here because I have to be."

He smirked and shook his head. "Senna, Senna, Senna. You don't seem to understand that you don't have a say in this matter."

Please.

I didn't get to this point in my life by letting douchebags get the better of me.

I stood, letting my popcorn spill all over the floor. "Go fuck yourself."

He tried to grab my hand, but I was too fast. I headed for the stairs to get back up to the concourse. The night was over.

And on my way up my interminable climb, who did I see in the *good seats*, but Chase Baldwyn.

Shit.

I hung my head and started taking the steps two at a time, finally reaching the top, out of breath and sweaty.

I had to get the hell out of there. I looked in every direction once I'd reached the concourse, trying to figure out which way the exit was.

I saw a sign with an arrow and headed toward it. But as soon as I did, Chase appeared right in front of me.

"Oh!"

"Hey, Senna. Are you okay?" he asked, concerning crossing his face.

"I... I'm not sure. I have to get out of here," I said in a trembling voice, looking around in a panic.

What the hell was wrong with me? Sure, I'd just climbed a shitload of steps, but my chest was tighter than if someone were sitting on it.

"C'mon," Chase said, taking my hand. "I'll drive you home."

As soon as the night air hit my face, I began to feel some relief.

"Are you gonna tell me what's going on?" he asked.

I looked behind us, and then all around to make sure Ty hadn't followed me. "It's a sordid story. And embarrassing. This jerk in my English class, I guess he's some kind of football star, told me that if I didn't go on a date with him, that he'd tell the university that I worked at Club V."

Chase stopped in his tracks. "He said *what*?"

My lower lip began to tremble, dammit. I never cried, and if I did, it was certainly not in front of anybody else. "He's blackmailing me. He said all I needed to do was go to the game with him tonight. That was the deal. But when we were sitting down there on the floor, he told me this wasn't the end of it."

I left out the part about writing his paper. The date was bad enough.

Chase opened the passenger door of his Jeep and helped me in, then hustled around to the driver's side.

"I can't... I don't know what to do..." I said, burying my face in my hands and letting the sobs take over.

"Oh, Senna. I'm so sorry," he said, rubbing my back.

"I...I'm sorry Chase. I d-didn't mean to d-dump this on you."

He started the car. "Where do you live? I'm taking you home."

By the time we arrived in front of my apartment building, I'd pretty much composed myself, although there was no doubt my face was a red, raw mess.

But I didn't care because I knew Chase didn't care.

"Do you want to come in?" I asked in a small voice, surprising us both.

I knew it probably wasn't the right thing to do, but I wanted some company. Actually, I wanted Chase's company. He made me feel safe, something I was desperate for after being with the horrible Ty—a monster who had no qualms about hurting me, and who relished in the knowledge that he could get away with it.

He turned the car off. "Yeah. Yeah, I do want to come in."

I took his hand and led him to my little studio apartment, which I'd decorated with great care. It was small, but it was the first place I'd ever lived alone, and I was in love with it.

"Wow. Cozy," he said, looking around appreciatively.

"I'm sorry it's not bigger. But it's home."

"Are you fucking kidding me? You know what my digs were like when I was in the Peace Corps? Let's just say I would have killed for a place like this back then. It's pure luxury."

He knew what to say to make me feel better. Not a lot of people had that skill.

I took him by the hand, leading him to my bed. I slowly lifted my T-shirt over my head and pushed my jeans to the floor. As I stood there in my mismatched black bra and pink panties, he smiled at me, his arms hanging at his sides. He wanted to see what I'd do next.

So I lifted his shirt off, and opened his blue jeans. He took hold of my shoulders, laying me back on the bed, where he slid between my legs with only my panties and his boxers separating our sexes.

"You know how long I've dreamed about doing this with you, Senna?"

I just smiled at him. He was amazing.

He pushed aside the crotch of my panties and lowered himself until I could feel his warm breath on my pussy. Shivers shot up my spine, and I could swear the room moved around us.

His tongue flicked me, and I gasped loudly. Groaning, he did it again, this time driving between my swollen lips.

"Oh fuck, that feels good," I murmured.

Cripes, he'd only just gotten started, and I was already a puddle of mush.

Running his tongue through my slit from top to bottom, he paused at my opening and then again on my clit. He pulled it into his mouth with a light suction.

That was all I needed. I writhed under his expert touch, pushing myself deeper into his mouth. Gripping the bed sheets for purchase, I threw my head back and forth on my pillow, gasping for air, my breathing raspy and deep.

"Oh god, yeah. I'm coming. I'm coming," I whispered as an orgasm slammed into me, leaving me convulsing from Chase's sexy ministrations.

Holy. Shit.

I finally opened my eyes to find him just looking at me.

"Are you ready for more?" he asked.

I laughed lightly. "I don't know. Are you?"

32

BENNO

DAMN IF OUR BUDDY CHASE HADN'T HAD SOME SEXY time with Senna. Not that he'd explicitly told me anything, but when he'd texted both Jamie and me, it was the middle of the night and there was no way he'd be up that late unless he was with her.

guys. mind if I invite senna out on the boat Sunday?

It was fine with me. In fact, more than fine. And I knew Jamie would feel the same way.

And now here we were, at the marina with two coolers and Senna in tow, looking fucking adorable with a scarf tied over her hair and in her cut offs and Converse low tops.

Damn. Not a stitch of makeup on her face and she

was even more gorgeous than the first time I met her dancing her heart out at Club V.

On the narrow walkway between boats, Senna stopped dead in her tracks when I pointed out Jamie's boat. Or, should I say, yacht. I was not good with boating vocabulary.

"What the…?" she cried. "*This* is your boat, Jamie?"

I kind of missed her calling us 'professor.' Something about it was so damn naughty.

Jamie caught up to us and slung an arm around her shoulder. I had to admit, they looked good together.

"It sure as hell is mine," he said, smiling at his pride and joy, which he'd geekily named 'School's Out.'

That was a professor for you.

Senna's feet were glued in place. "Um, how… how did you get a boat like this? You're a university professor. Did you rob a bank?" She looked at him suspiciously.

Yeah, she had a lot to learn about Jamie.

"C'mon," he said, pulling her by the hand. "I'll tell you everything."

I couldn't deny I felt a little pang of something I couldn't put into words when I saw Jamie so at ease with Senna, taking her by the hand and laughing as they headed toward the boat.

While I was down with, on a intellectual level, with the concept of sharing a woman, I knew I had some soul-searching to do to see if this was the right kind of arrangement for me.

Shit, we didn't even know if Senna was really down with it, truth be told.

Everything was up in the air—a status I've never been comfortable with. I liked to know what was coming at me, at least to the best extent I could. I didn't leave much to chance. But I was going to roll with things as best I could.

At least Jamie and Chase were chill about it all.

I got on the boat and stored my things in the same cupboard I used every time we went out on School's Out. Chase followed me into the cabin, dropping his stuff next to the captain's chair, where he planted himself.

He grabbed the steering wheel like a little kid in Dad's car. "Dude, I am so ready for this. A little sun, some fresh air, salt water. Just what the doctor ordered."

I wish I could be as easy going as he was. But I guess when you've spent years in the Peace Corps, you learn to be pretty damn adaptable.

He reached for Senna's waist and pulled her to him, kissing her while running a hand over her shorts and grabbing a fistful of her ass. When she dropped her head back and giggled, he ran his lips over her neck.

I had to say, in spite of my misgivings—if that's what you could call them—it was hot as shit to see how they reacted to each other. I just hoped she'd have some left for me.

"Hey, out of my seat," Jamie said, elbowing Chase out of the captain's chair.

Chase jumped out of the way, leading Senna to the front of the boat. "You have to let me drive later, then," he called over his shoulder.

Jamie looked at me and rolled his eyes. "Like he could maneuver out of the marina. That guy's hilarious."

I stood next to Jamie as he got the boat out of its small slip and then traveled past all the other yachts to get to the open ocean. "It always amazes me how good you are at this."

He laughed. "I have to be. You know how much this boat cost? She's my baby," he said, patting the dashboard. "I'd never let anything happen to her."

We hugged the coast for a while, with Senna and Chase canoodling on the front of the boat. I was watching them with one eye and trying to learn some of the boat's controls with the other.

"See," Jamie said, "if you learn how to pilot the boat, you can kick me off in the middle of the ocean and keep School's Out for yourself."

"How'd you know that's exactly what I had in mind?" I asked, cuffing him on the shoulder.

As soon as Jamie cut the engines, I opened an icy bottle of champagne and found four plastic flutes.

"Guys," I yelled, "time for a toast."

Senna and Chase came bounding into the cabin, their faces flushed and their hair wild from the wind.

"Champagne, yum," Senna squealed, taking the glass I'd handed her.

She and Chase had stripped down to their bathing suits. Senna's was a shiny one-piece that looked like a second skin. It was very high cut over the ass, revealing most of her round cheeks, and tied behind her neck with a crisscross over the front to cover her tits.

I couldn't take my eyes off her.

I held my glass up. "I want to toast my good friends and welcome Senna to our exclusive little club."

"I'm glad to hear it's exclusive. If I thought you did this with every college girl, that would kind of suck."

Everyone laughed and sipped their champagne.

"C'mere baby," I said. I couldn't keep my hands off her any longer.

She gave me a wicked look and sauntered over.

I met her defiant gaze and let my hand travel down the front of her suit until it landed on her breast. I rubbed my open palm on the thin fabric until her nipple was stiff. With our gazes locked, I pulled her flesh between my thumb and forefinger.

She winced, but only for a second. So I did it harder.

"Oh," she sighed, her eyes closing halfway.

Jamie and Chase nodded at me while adjusting themselves in the crotch department.

I had a bit of adjusting to do myself, but I wasn't about to take my hands off my girl.

Shit. *My girl?*

Fuck, was I in trouble.

I inched aside the small strip of fabric covering Senna's pussy and burrowed between her lips to find her slick with excitement. I pulled my hand back to taste her.

Heaven.

While I worked her breast and pussy, Chase came over and turned her head just enough to kiss her, their lips licking and sucking each other's right in front of me.

That left Jamie, never one to be left out.

I drove a finger inside Senna while I worked her clit. She moaned into Chase's mouth while Jamie came up behind her and untied the fabric around her neck. The top half of her suit fell toward the floor, and he reached around her from behind to play with her firm tits.

With all three of us guys working her over, she swayed between us with the rocking of the boat, getting lost in the intense sensation of having every inch of her body touched—worshipped, really.

"I'm going to fuck you, darling," I said in her ear.

She didn't say a thing. Just looked at me and nodded.

Chase peeled the rest of her bathing suit down to the floor and there she stood, beautiful and naked for the three of us, one hand holding Jamie for balance, the other holding me.

I pulled a condom out of my pocket, and dropping my pants and boxers, quickly sheathed myself.

"C'mon," I said, quietly.

I sat on the bench seat with my dick raging hard, ready to fuck the shit out of this beauty.

She started to straddle me where I sat, but I stopped her.

"No. Turn around. I want the other guys to see you."

With a bit of balancing, she faced away and climbed on me backward for a sort of reverse cowgirl. This way, she had to lean forward a bit, which provided a perfect view of my cock against her opening as well as her pink asshole. I put my hands on her waist, and slowly drew her onto me.

Jamie and Chase in the meantime had dropped their bathing suits, each offering their hard dicks to Senna, which she greedily took. First, she sucked Chase while she stroked Jamie and then switched, just like she had with Jamie and me that day in his office.

But when I began to pull her back and forth on my cock with more speed, her head dropped back, and she grabbed her tits.

"Fuck me. God, fuck me harder, please," she breathed, her breath coming fast and hard.

Chase kissed her hard. Jamie reached down to play with her clit as I slid in and out.

Oh fuck, I was going to come, too.

"Goddamn," I bellowed, pulling her down so hard on me my balls were up against her pussy.

"Oh, oh," she moaned, thrashing through her orgasm. "Yeah, fuck me like that...." she screamed.

Her whole body trembled while she came, and continued to for what seemed like forever. I held her while I watched my cock slide in and out of her wet pussy.

As soon as she was somewhat lucid again, she pulled Chase's dick into her mouth and sucked him all the way to the root. Jamie's cock was in her hand, which she stroked with a vengeance.

And I sat back, still inside her tight pussy, watching her work over my friends. Just as Chase started to come in her mouth, Jamie spurted all over her pretty tits.

"Fucking A," I said. "This is what I call a good day on the boat."

33

BENNO

THERE WAS A KNOCK ON MY OFFICE DOOR. I GLANCED AT my watch. I wasn't expecting anyone, but then during office hours, students often dropped in unannounced.

I was trying to grade my Freshman English class's papers, but I'd been unable to focus, thinking all day about Senna and the three of us guys out on the boat the day before. Mondays were always rough, but today was really killing me.

I liked Senna. A lot. And the guys did, too. And after watching her with all of us, I was more comfortable with the idea of sharing. To be honest, seeing her with the other guys was one of the fucking hottest things I'd ever experienced.

I pulled my office door open, and my spirits sank to the depth of my shoes.

"Krishelle. What are you doing here?"

She'd caught me by such surprise that I couldn't even pretend to be glad to see her. It was never a happy occasion when she came around, and I braced myself for whatever shit she had to throw my way.

But I wasn't expecting what she had for me that day.

"Hello, Benjamin," she said, helping herself to a seat before I could offer her one.

She looked around my office, perhaps warming up for whatever poison she had to share. When her gaze returned to me, she narrowed her eyes, lizard-like. "I'm going to get right to the point."

I shrugged. "When have you ever *not* gotten right to the point?" I asked.

My effort to lighten the tension was lost on her.

"I know you've been with Senna Duncan."

She sat back in her chair, arms crossed, looking proud of herself.

My adrenaline surged as several mangled thoughts ran through my head.

I could deny it and tell her she was full of shit.

I could probe a bit to see where she'd gotten her information.

Or I could own up to it.

We were adults. We could theoretically do what we

wanted. The line between student-teacher relationships was fuzzy. The university advised against them, but left such things to the discretion of the adults involved.

Did she know about Jamie and Chase, as well? And how the hell would she have found out, anyway?

I decided to blow her mind.

"Yes, I have. She and I are dating."

Well, she clearly hadn't expected me to be honest, because her head snapped back, and her mouth fell open.

She was a horrid, horrid woman. She'd stalked me on numerous occasions, with some crazy idea that if I just got to know her, we'd have a relationship. I hoped to god she wasn't back to that now. It had been stressful the last time. I'd been forced to bring in the university's administration, which reluctantly sanctioned her so I wouldn't notify the police.

Thanks, Wellshire.

Her fingers gripped the arms of her chair so hard they were turning white. "I can report you. You can lose your job."

God, she was a fucking loon.

"You can report me, Krishelle. That's true."

I stood and pulled my office door open. "Now, if you're done, I'd like you to leave. I have work to do," I said calmly.

She pursed her lips, her angry face red with the

humiliation of my dismissal. "This isn't the last you're going to hear of this," she hissed, and passed through my doorway. She turned to face me. "And if you think you're—"

I slammed my door right in her face. I'd had enough.

Fine. I was seeing a student. I wasn't the first person at the university to do that, and I certainly wouldn't be the last. I just had to prepare myself for any potential fallout.

But how did she find out? And on the other hand, did it really matter? The point was, she *had* found out.

Would she really tell the administration, though? She'd come to me, wanting something. And if I knew her as well as I thought, she'd be back.

Just then, there was another knock on my door. Christ, she hadn't waited long.

I swung it open. "Look, I really need you to—"

But I stopped myself.

It wasn't Krishelle.

It was Ty Duvall, the idiot football player from Freshman English.

"Oh. Ty. Come in," I said, opening the door for him.

"Hey, Professor Adler. How's it shaking?" he asked with his big, dumb smile.

"I'm well, Ty. What's going on?"

I wanted to get him out of there as quickly as I could.

"Well, I figured I'd stop by and see how I did on my

biography assignment. Hoping I got an A, but you never know, do you?"

I doubt he'd ever gotten an A in anything.

And he certainly hadn't on this assignment.

I shuffled through the papers on my desk and pulled his from the bottom, holding so he couldn't see it.

"First, Ty, I was surprised to see that Taylor Swift was the topic of your bio. That was unexpected. But I enjoyed learning about such a huge pop star. I hadn't really known much about her."

Confusion crossed his face as my snarkiness went right over his head. "You mean Kanye, right? Kanye's the one I like."

If this guy were any more of a cliché, it would have been funny rather than sad.

I handed him his five-page paper. His eyes bugged out and red washed over his face.

"What the fuck, dude?" he asked in a raised voice.

Great. Two psychos in one day.

"You failed the assignment, Ty. But I'm willing to offer you the opportunity to write a new paper. Maybe this time you could focus on Kanye." I couldn't help throwing that dig at him.

He waved his paper around in front of him. "This is bullshit. You can't give me an F."

I sat back in my seat and nodded. "I can, and I did."

He raked his fingers through his hair, clearly unused to not getting his way. "I don't know how this could have come out so badly," he said, flipping through the pages' red marks.

"Ty, it sounds like you didn't even write the paper."

His head snapped up. "I didn't. Senna Duncan wrote it for me."

34

SENNA

"Senna, do you have a moment?"

Oh, yeah. Always for my hot English professor. I couldn't wait to hear his feedback on my biography on Maugham. I thought I'd really nailed it.

Or maybe he wanted to discuss something a little more… sexy?

Benno waited for the last student to leave the room before he looked from his phone. And when he did, his eyes were dark in a way I'd never seen them. And tired.

He started by shaking his head. "I cannot begin to tell you how pissed I am that you wrote Ty Duvall's paper."

Oh. Shit.

My stomach dropped to the depths of both fear and shame unlike anything I'd experienced in a long time.

Like the first time I brought a friend over after my dad died. My mom was on her way to losing her shit, but I didn't know that yet. The progression was insidious, and it was probably a year or two after his death that I realized Mom was gone, replaced by a stranger. And that I was pretty much on my own.

"What are you doing here?" she'd growled from the living room sofa when we came in. I was old enough to know she'd been drinking. A lot.

Thus the humiliation.

I showed my friend out the back door and told her I'd see her in school the next morning. When I came back inside, my mother screamed at me until I ran to my room and locked the door. I slept in the closet that night.

And my friend never spoke to me again.

Although the circumstances were completely different right now, facing Benno, the same sensations were running through me. I sniffed hard to keep the tears back.

Shit. Second time in one week I'd cried. What the fuck was wrong with me?

"I... I can explain, Benno—"

He moved closer to me and lowered his voice. "If it were anybody else, Senna, you'd be kicked out of school. I have an obligation to turn you in, but I'm not going to."

One little tear dribbled down my cheek. But I held my head up, trying to chase away the shame.

"Benno... Benno, you have to let me explain," I pleaded, grabbing his arm.

He just looked at me.

"That Ty, he's a horrible person, Benno. He's extorting me, making me do favors for him or else he'll get me in trouble with the university for working at Club V."

He snapped his head back. "Are you fucking kidding?"

"Benno, I'm so sorry I didn't tell you sooner. I... I didn't know what to do, so I went along with what he wanted."

His eyes got dark. Really dark. "What did he ask of you?"

I swallowed. "F... first he said I had to write a paper for him. I did a lousy job to get even. And I had to go on a date with him. We went to a game, but I left early. I couldn't stand it. But before I took off, he said I had to go on other dates with him—" My voice caught and all the craziness in my life suddenly felt like it was sitting on my chest.

I reached for a chair. "I... I need to sit down..."

"Here," he said, helping me to a seat. "Calm down. We're going to figure this out."

He paced the classroom like a caged lion ready to pounce. "I'm going to fucking kill that punk. That's all there is to it."

I glanced out to the hallway as I willed my dizziness away. People were passing by in hordes, but no one was paying any attention to us.

"You know who I got a call from this morning?" Benno asked. "The fucking football coach. He told me to lay off Ty. I told him he had to be kidding. That kid is a fucking loser, I told him. He doesn't deserve to be here at Wellshire. For Christ's sake, he's in his third year here and still hasn't made it through Freshman English. I hate this shit. I hate it…" His voice tapered off as he ran his hands through his hair in frustration.

"Wow. The coach can do that?" I asked.

If what Benno was saying were true, the academic world was certainly not what I'd thought it was.

He continued walking back and forth. "They do shit like that all the time. Everybody knows about it, but little is said or done about it."

"Why do they protect guys like him?"

"Because they bring in money. Sell tickets to games, raise the profile of the university, make the coaches look good. They don't care about Ty per se. They just care about what he can do for them. They'd push him through his undergrad degree even if he didn't know how to fucking read."

He stopped pacing and stood in front of me. "I can understand why you did it. But if you have any more issues like this, you come tell me right away. Understand?"

I nodded. I hadn't imagined being caught, and I

certainly hadn't imagined Benno losing his shit like he had. If Ty happened by at that very moment, Benno probably would have torn his head off.

"Thank you for listening to my side of the story. I gotta run now. I have my shift at the fitness center."

"Okay, get going. But we're all having dinner together tonight, right?"

I gave him a limp smile. "Yeah. Unless you don't want to anymore."

He helped me to my feet and after a quick glance around kissed my cheek.

"Oh, I want to see you tonight. Very much," he whispered in my ear.

35

SENNA

As soon as my shift at the fitness center was over, I bolted from campus and went home. I was shaken by my conversation with Benno, but also excited to see all the guys together again. Hopefully, there would be no tension to ruin the night.

Would he tell the other guys about my writing Ty's paper? I couldn't bear the shame, but on the other hand, I was committed to being honest with them. I wasn't proud of what I'd done, but they should know. They wouldn't think less of me when they heard the whole story.

Jamie had suggested dinner at one of the nicest restaurants in town, so I'd borrowed a black halter-top jumpsuit from Godiva and paired it with some strappy high heels. It was a simple outfit but elegant. I ironed my hair straight and carefully applied a very natural makeup look, which I finished with a dark red lipstick.

I checked myself out in the mirror and liked what I saw. I was sexy without looking like I was trying hard, something that was not easy to accomplish.

Thirty minutes later, an Uber dropped me at the restaurant. The maître d' was waiting, and personally took me to the table where the guys were sitting.

As I approached, I slowed my walk. I wanted time to look each of them in the eye and let them know how special they were becoming to me.

And of course, I wanted to give them time to check me out, too.

"Holy shit," Jamie said, jumping up to pull my chair out. As I took my seat, he leaned down and kissed my ear. "You are stunning, baby."

He walked around the other side of the table and settled in across from me, leaving me sitting between Benno and Chase.

I leaned toward Benno for a quick peck.

"Hello, stranger," he laughed.

And then I turned to Chase, who put his hands on either side of my face and kissed me passionately.

"Hey Senna, you have a French test coming up," he said.

I smiled. "Do you think you might be available to help me study?" I flirted.

He reached under the table and took my hand. "Anytime, darlin'."

Jamie reached into a bucket and poured me a glass of champagne, then one for himself and the guys. "Cheers," he said, and we all clinked glasses.

I looked around the table at three impossibly gorgeous men—Benno with his messy shock of hair and nerd glasses, Jamie with his dimples and bicep tattoos, and Chase with his heavy dark brow and small ponytail.

Jesus, had I died and gone to heaven? Because it sure felt like it.

The tension between Benno and me earlier in the day seemed to have been set aside, at least for the moment, as we talked and laughed and chose delicious things off the menu. I'd never had escargot, which Chase convinced me to try.

The guys were all so special to me in different ways. God, I loved being with them.

Shit, did I say *love*?

"So, Senna, there is something we want to talk to you about," Jamie started.

I looked around at the three of them. "Okay. Let me have it."

Chase continued. "We want to make our little arrangement a bit more formal."

Formal? What the hell did that mean?

"What we're saying, Senna," Benno said, "is that we

want to share you in a long-term sort of way. Like you'd be girlfriend to all of us."

My stomach did a flip.

Geez. I hadn't thought about what we were all doing beyond a day or two into the future. But it sure seemed like the guys had.

"Wow. Just wow," I said, trying to get my jumbled thoughts straight. "I'm not sure what that means, but it sounds intriguing."

Out of nervousness, I took a too-big gulp of champagne, catching the dribble that landed on my chin with a finger.

Smooth.

Luckily, before anyone could expect me to answer, the waiter arrived with our meals.

Jamie held his hands up. "Just think about it. No need to make any decisions now."

I was so honored. No matter which direction things went in, I loved that these guys thought enough of me to welcome me into their lives.

I broke off a piece of my halibut, and with my bite halfway to my mouth, was interrupted by a familiar voice.

"Well, look who we have here."

"Krishelle. Hello. I'd say it was nice to see you, but I try not to lie," Benno said between gritted teeth.

I whipped around to see my academic advisor standing right behind me, her eyes narrowed, and her mouth twisted with disgust.

This was not going to be good.

I set my fork down and turned in my chair. "Ms. Abalone. Hello."

She looked me up and down like I was covered in dirt. "Senna, what are you doing with these men?" she spat.

"Krishelle, I don't think—" Benno began.

But I cut him off. I could handle my shit. "Why do you ask?"

My hands clenched into fists so tight my fingernails cut my palms. This woman had been horrible to me since day one, and I was about done putting up with it.

She glared at me. "You know why I'm asking."

I shrugged. "Do you ask everyone you see in a restaurant *why* they are there? Seems kind of silly to me." I laughed.

Her face went from pink to red and she looked at Benno. "You... you're going to have to answer for this—"

But I cut her off. "Look, Krishelle, we'd ask you to sit down and have a seat with us"—her eyes bulged as I addressed her by her first name—"but... we don't have any more room."

I turned back to my plate and ate the bite of halibut that was still on my fork. I closed my eyes to enjoy the buttery fish and to try to get Ms. Abalone's hateful face out of my mind. When I opened my eyes, the guys were looking over my shoulder, watching her retreat.

"Jesus Christ," Chase said. "You actually chased off the witch."

I looked at Benno and Jamie, who were stifling laughter.

I had to smile, too. It had felt great to goad that nasty woman.

"Oh my god, I never thought I'd see someone get the last word on her," Benno said, now shaking with laughter.

"Senna, hats off to you. That was fucking awesome," Jamie said.

I shrugged. A girl could only put up with so much shit. "But Benno, what did she mean you were going to have to answer for something?"

Shifting in his chair, he looked down at the table for a moment, then shrugged. "I don't know. Must be something about back when she was stalking me. She's a psycho."

Well, first thing on my list for tomorrow was to try to get a new academic advisor. There was no doubt my smart-assed remarks had sealed my fate with Ms. Abalone.

And the second thing on my list was to think about the guys' offer.

36

JAMIE

AFTER OUR EVENTFUL DINNER, WE ALL HEADED OVER TO Club V. Not because Senna had to work, but because the club was having a private party for its regular members. Every dancer got to invite a few of her favorites.

And Senna had chosen us three guys.

I was looking forward to it. I really was. There would be no entertainment, per se—it wasn't about that. It was more a chance for the dancers to mingle with some of the club's long-standing regulars and, I guess, make them feel appreciated. An awesome idea, if you asked me.

"Godiva, this is Benno, Jamie, and Chase," she said

to a lovely little blonde I'd seen dancing there before, and who came rushing up to us the moment we arrived.

Beaming, she bounced up and down in her long silvery gown. "I've heard so much about all of you."

She had?

"Now, which one is which?" she asked, tapping her chin and scrutinizing us.

Senna dropped her head back and laughed as a waitress thrust overflowing champagne flutes in each of our hands.

"Guess, Godiva. See if you can figure it out," she said.

We guys smiled at each other. Did I look like anything other than a math teacher? Shit, I hoped so. I didn't have a pocket protector or my pants pulled up to my chin.

"Hmmm. Now let me see."

She took a couple steps back, then walked behind us, looking us up and down.

"I feel like a piece of meat," Benno fake-whined.

Senna burst out laughing again. "Godiva, just guess! It's not like there's a prize or anything."

Godiva raised an eyebrow at Senna, who shrugged knowingly.

There *was* a prize. For Senna, anyway.

"Okay," Godiva said after a sip of champagne, "you are the English teacher," she said, pointing at Chase.

Strike one.

She looked at Senna. "Am I right?"

Senna shrugged. "Keep going. You're not done."

Godiva rolled her eyes. "Some friend you are. Not even helping me," she said dramatically.

"You've chosen the English teacher. Now choose Math and French," Chase said, laughing.

"You," she said, pointing at me, "are the French teacher. And you" —she pointed at Benno— "are the Math teacher."

Strikes two and three.

Senna jumped up and down with delight. God, she was cute.

"Godiva, darling, you got them all wrong," Senna said.

She frowned, then laughed. "Well, it doesn't matter. All that matters is that you guys have a good time."

And she skittered off into the crowd.

We followed Senna into the heart of the party, where beautiful women chatted with their favorite customers and everyone was smiling and engaged. A few ladies were dancing on the stage with men—not entertaining, just dancing—and over in a corner two women were showing a bunch of guys some of their moves so they could give exotic dancing a try. From where I stood, it was a hysterical performance of awkward clumsiness.

"Well, hello," a tall reed of a woman with mannishly cropped hair said, extending her hand.

Senna's eyes brightened. "Guys, this is Zin, the owner of Club V. And my boss, of course."

"Nice to see you gentlemen. Thank you for being good customers, and for taking such good care of our girl here," she said, gesturing toward Senna.

I didn't know what I'd expected the party to be, but it had a warm, happy feel to it. All the ladies were charming, and the men entirely respectful. But then, it was a private party, and they weren't about to include difficult or asshole customers.

"You guys want to see the dressing room? Where all the magic happens?" Senna asked with a twinkle in her eyes.

She led us to a room that would have been dingy if not for racks of colorful costumes and Styrofoam heads holding an assortment of wigs. Bright lights shone above a row of tables, cluttered with more makeup and glitter than I thought could be used in a lifetime.

"This is cool as shit," Chase said, turning around and taking it all in. "Oh, and dude," he said, clapping Benno on the back, "sorry I stole 'English teacher' from you. You got math. That's freaking hilarious."

"What's so funny about being a math teacher?" I asked in my best stern voice.

Chase's eyebrows rose. "Oh, sorry, Jamie. It's just that everyone knows math people are nerds."

Well. He was pretty much right.

But still.

Just then, the dressing room door flew open, and a woman in a slinky yellow dress bounded through the door, followed by a guy whose hand she was holding.

"Oh!" she said. "Didn't know anyone would be in here."

Senna stepped next to her. "Guys, this is Sadie. Sadie, this is Benno, Jamie, and Chase."

She gave us a brilliant smile. I thought she looked familiar, but without the makeup, wigs, and costumes, most of the women were unrecognizable. But no less beautiful.

"Oh, hi," Sadie said. "This is my boyfriend Morrison. I think we'll leave you guys to it," she added, winking at Senna, and taking off.

When she was gone, I said, "Leave us to *what*? What did she mean?"

I sat my ass on the dressing table behind me and took Senna's hand, gently pulling her to me. I positioned her between my thighs and spun her until her back was to me. I'd been staring at her bare neck all night and I was desperate to get my lips on it.

And as soon as I pushed her hair aside to press them to her warm skin, she sighed, letting her head drop to give me better access.

I glanced at the grinning Chase and Benno, who made themselves comfortable, watching us, grateful I'd turned Senna toward them.

As I kissed her neck, my hands wandered, where I found her breasts under the silky fabric of her jumpsuit. She was braless, something that had been driving me crazy all night, because every time she moved, her firm tits jiggled just the right amount.

"How's that, baby?" I asked quietly, relishing the feel of her in my hands.

She tilted her head to give me the other side of her neck. "So good," she murmured.

I gently tugged on the wide bow behind her neck, and her top slithered down to her waist, baring beautiful tits. Chase and Benno shifted where they sat, most certainly getting painfully hard in their trousers just like I was.

Over her shoulder, I watched her scoop her breasts together. Her nipples were full and pink with tips now as hard as little rocks. I pulled her closer to grind my cock against her ass, rolling her nipples between my fingers.

"God, Jamie," she said on a long breath.

She about-faced, her tits bouncing out of my hands, and began to yank on my belt buckle and fly. Reaching inside my trousers, she pushed down my boxers, grabbing for my aching cock.

Stroking me from tip to balls and back, she lingered on my cockhead to smear my precum into the palm of her hand and pressed her lips to mine.

Her kiss was different, hungry, demanding—almost aggressive. And it turned me on like nothing I'd ever experienced.

Here she was, a beautiful smart woman, enjoying her sexuality without reservation.

And while I was relishing her kiss, with a quick movement, she opened wide and began deep throating me with her pretty mouth. She had a little trouble with my girth, but managed to take as much of me as she could handle. Moving up and down on my erection, her tits swung back and forth, almost causing me to shoot my load in seconds.

But I wanted to make it last. I leaned my hands back on the table where I sat, getting fucking glitter all over myself, spreading my legs as far as my half-on half-off trousers would permit, and pushed myself between her lips.

"Fuck, baby. Goddamn," I growled.

Chase walked up behind Senna to stroke her tits from behind. He leaned toward her ear. "Can I fuck you, beautiful?" he whispered.

With a mouthful of my cock, she couldn't speak. So, she nodded, moaning. Chase lowered her jumpsuit and then her thong panty, and spread her legs wide enough to wedge himself between them.

Reaching in his pocket, he produced a condom, and as soon as he had his jeans open, he covered himself and positioned his dick at the opening of her pussy.

While he was doing this, Senna continued to bob up and down on my cock, alternately running her tongue around my explosively sensitive head, and then taking me nearly up to my balls.

"Oh," she groaned, pulling her mouth off me, and pushing back toward Chase until he was all the way in. "Yeah."

She lowered herself once again on my dick, and when Chase started to bang away, her head bounced against my stomach.

"Oh fuck, baby," I growled. I knew I wasn't going to last long.

With one last dive down my shaft, Senna received my cum like she was thirsting for it, swallowing as fast as she could. She licked off me what was left.

Resting her head in my lap, I held her arms while Chase pummeled the shit out of her from behind. His face was red, his eyes closed and lips pressed together in pure concentration. Senna's moans built until she was thrashing her head and bucking back on him to get a deeper fuck.

"Oh, oh," she moaned. "Yeah, I'm coming."

The beautiful sounds of our girl orgasming filled the room, quickly followed by Chase's own bellowing noises.

Senna was nearly worn out, but Benno took her by the arms and lowered her to her knees. He grabbed his cock, which he'd pulled out of his pants at some point, and with a final couple jerks, spurted his cum all over her tits.

From her kneeling position, Senna looked up at us, dazed, her hair a tangled mess, and a smudge of mascara under one eye.

She was perfect.

We gently settled her into a chair and cleaned her up, at least enough to make her presentable. Chase held her jumpsuit open and Benno guided her legs into it while I helped her remain upright. Glitter had somehow worked its way onto all of us, and it became apparent that trying to brush it off was a losing battle. When Senna was ready, she took the bottle of water I'd handed her and dressed, sat back in her chair, wiped out.

"Are you gonna make it, baby?" Chase asked with a smile.

She nodded, clearly happy. At least I thought she was.

Standing, she surprised us all by making her way to the door. "Guys," she started, looking at each of us, "thank you. Thank you for your friendship. Thank you for the fun we've had. But I can't be with you. I just can't. I don't feel right about it. Someone will get hurt. I know it," she said, her voice breaking.

She dashed out the door, leaving it open, and leaving us three guys staring at each other like the assholes that we were.

37

SENNA

"Hey, Senna."

I knew that voice. And it turned my stomach.

As if I didn't already feel shitty enough.

I looked up from the fitness center's front desk to take Ty's ID.

I didn't say a word, just ran his card through the scanner, handed it back, and returned to studying my French flash cards. I figured if I ignored him long enough, he'd go away.

I was wrong.

"Hey, I wanted to tell you I accidentally told Professor Adler you wrote my English paper for me."

I continued sorting my cards and didn't look up. "I know."

"Yeah. You might be getting in trouble for that. It's a shame. It just kind of slipped out of my mouth when I was pissed. He's such a dick, isn't he?"

Was there a baseball bat nearby that I could slug him with? I was in a fitness center, after all.

"You're not getting in trouble for it?" I asked, finally looking up at his smug face.

He shrugged. "'Course not. I mean, Adler tried to get me in trouble, but the coach told him to back off. Teachers like that don't understand what football brings to this university."

How did such a lame human being get to be so arrogant?

Too nauseated to say anything else, I turned back to my cards.

He drummed his fingers on the counter.

Shit, where was Patti when I needed her? I craned my neck to see through the giant window to her office, but she had her back turned to it, talking to somebody else.

"I was thinking, Senna, that our next date could be—"

That was all I could take. I snapped.

"Are you fucking *kidding me*? I'm not going *anywhere* with you, *ever*," I hissed.

He tilted his head and smiled. "Now that's too bad. A real shame. Because when the university finds out what you do for a living, and I don't mean sitting here on your ass in the fitness center three days a week, they'll run you out so fast you won't know what hit you."

Bastard.

"Just think, all the work you've done so far this semester will have been a total waste. All the money you spent for tuition, down the drain."

Would they really kick me out? Or was he bluffing?

God fucking dammit. As if I didn't already have enough on my mind, namely three gorgeous professors named Benno, Jamie, and Chase, not to mention that horrendous excuse for an academic advisor, Krishelle Abalone.

Did I really need some dumb fuck jock getting in my face?

C'mon universe. Throw me a bone.

"Do what you need to do, Ty. You're the one who has to live with yourself."

He laughed. "Sure, babe. Suit yourself. You know, you're not that hot anyway. *Bitch*."

Ah, *bitch*. Men wielded that word like it was their most precious weapon, doling it out because they knew the penalty for striking us any other way was so severe. But I knew a few things about men, and I knew that the ones who used that word were the most damaged. After I'd emerged from the rage that being called a bitch usually filled me with, I found I actually had pity for those men. They'd never gain the respect of a woman, which was what they wanted more than anything.

Ty he sauntered away, waving to the other gym-goers like he was the superstar he imagined he was.

Was my college career really that close to being over? A lump grew in my throat as I thought about it. I'd had such high hopes for Wellshire and myself. Never did I think I'd get embroiled with such hateful people.

But never did I think I'd meet three such amazing men.

Fuck.

Should I tell them about Ty's threat? Could it pose any danger to them or their careers? I couldn't see how, and yet I felt the need to give them a heads up.

"Senna!" Patti said, sauntering toward me.

Where had she been two minutes ago?

"Wow. That Ty Duvall really seems to like you, always chatting you up and stuff. How'd you get so lucky? You know how many women throw themselves at him?"

Thank god it was almost time for my shift to end.

"Yeah. I feel super lucky."

38

SENNA

I TURNED OVER IN BED AND REACHED FOR MY PHONE ON the nightstand. I'd tossed and turned all night, and figured it was time to just drag my ass out of bed and get my day started.

I had a new English paper to hand in, an exam in Math, and a vocabulary quiz in French. I'd even taken a few days off work at Club V to catch up with all my schoolwork. Those extra hours, plus not seeing any of the guys, had actually given me a nice chunk of time to really dig in to my classes. I wasn't living as if I were about to get kicked out of school, no matter what Ty said.

I was certain he was full of shit.

Right?

Ugh. Six a.m.

I pushed myself up, and scrolled through my overnight emails. And don't you know there was one from the lovely Krishelle Abalone.

Please stop by my office as soon as you can.

What the hell did she want, other than to harass me over something petty? I wasn't hanging out with the guys anymore, so she couldn't say a thing about them. In fact, I could even placate her by pretending I stopped being friends with them on her recommendation.

She was the type who flattery worked on. The one time I told her that her hair looked nice, she looked like she wanted to kiss me.

I emailed her right back.

Will stop by this morning.

I headed over to campus to catch Abalone before my first class. Might as well get it over with, rather than wonder all morning what the hell she wanted.

I knocked on her door, half-hoping she wouldn't be in. But I knew she would. She kept very early hours, god knew why. College students didn't do anything early in the morning unless they absolutely had to.

"Come in," she called.

I poked my head in the door. I wanted to make sure she didn't have any sharp objects lying around, especially after the way I'd spoken to her at the restaurant several nights back.

I took a seat without being invited. My heart was pounding, but I held my head up. I wasn't about to let her know she could scare me.

But in reality, she *was* fucking scary. And according to the guys, a nut job.

"See this morning's school paper?" she asked, shoving the skimpy tabloid toward me.

I didn't take it. "I don't read it. I'm not interested. Can you tell me why I'm here this morning, Ms. Abalone?"

She pursed her lips. "You might want to read the paper this time, Senna, because it has a story about you."

Fuck.

My stomach fell. Please don't let me get sick right here, right now. If it were going to happen, and I was pretty sure it would, I had to hold off until I got out of the crazy lady's office. So I couldn't look down at the paper. I just kept my gaze locked to Abalone's cold, black eyes.

"Read it," she demanded.

With a trembling hand, I slowly turned the paper around and looked at the first column, then the second. So far so good. What had she been talking about?

I found out when I reached the third column.

Student Makes Ends Meet Dancing at Club V was the headline. I didn't need to read more. I didn't have to. After all, I knew my own goddamn story.

Ty had gotten to someone on the paper in revenge

for my turning him down. He'd made good on his promise. He couldn't pull off passing Freshman English, but he could pitch an article to the student newspaper to inflict as much harm as he could on someone. Probably offered him free tickets to one of his games. Or popcorn.

What a waste of a human being.

I exhaled slowly to calm myself and returned my gaze to Abalone.

Why me? Seriously. Couldn't the universe give me a fucking break? There might have been some level of fairness in the world, but it sure had never rained down on me.

Ty was yet *another* person trying to make me feel worthless. When would they leave me alone? Who had I hurt?

And at that moment, all I wanted to do was talk to the guys.

My three guys.

"Aren't you going to read it, Senna?" she asked with a smirk.

"No. No, I'm not. And I have a busy day, so I'll head out now—" I started to stand.

"You need to leave the university. I have the withdrawal papers right here."

What?

What did she just say? Something about leaving? The university?

"Ms. Abalone, is this voluntary? Or am I being kicked out?"

"At this point it is voluntary. Which is why I'm suggesting it. If you wait for the university to do an investigation and then make it known that someone like you hurt their hard-earned reputation, you'll be ruined. By withdrawing, you can leave quietly without attracting any attention to yourself... or Professor Adler, whom you've been consorting with."

Wait. What?

"You don't deserve to be at Wellshire," she said matter-of-factly.

I didn't think I'd ever been so close to murder.

While I didn't accept a word the horrible woman was throwing my way, I'd be lying if barbs like that didn't sow seeds of doubt. Of course, the seeds of doubt had already been there. They had been for as long as I could remember. She'd just watered them nicely.

A strange pressure thumped in my chest. I wasn't sure whether it was anger at the shitty people who'd tried to hold me back or grief that they'd had the ability to do it. But it was explosive. And it wasn't going to stay there, neatly tucked away.

I had to get out.

But not without one last comment.

I signed the withdrawal papers Krishelle had shoved in front of me. My short-lived college career was over.

"You are a sad, sad woman, Ms. Abalone. I'll go on and one way or the other make a good life for myself. But you'll be stuck here in the knowledge that you can't ever do anything else or go anywhere because you are a limited human being."

All expression slipped from her face.

"*You* are the one who is nothing. And you always will be," I said.

I left, calmly pulling her door closed behind me.

And made it to the ladies' room just in time.

AFTER I'D CLEANED myself up and had some cold water, I lumbered outside the administration building and wandered into a small grove with an empty bench. Closing my eyes, I took deep breaths to smooth out my racing thoughts and heartbeat.

And as I pushed the ugliness of my conversation with Abalone into the far corners of my mind, all that surfaced in its place were the beautiful faces of Benno, Jamie, and Chase. Three sexy, smart, kind, and funny men who saw me as I was and had no reservations about me or my choices.

Had I ever known anyone, aside from Godiva, who'd supported me the way they did? I couldn't think of one, much less name one.

Then, what the fuck was I doing, telling them everything was over? I hadn't known them long, it was true. But every time we got together, there was something that just felt so right, like finding the exact piece in a huge puzzle you've been working on forever. I loved the loyal and easy friendship they shared, how different they were from each other, and yet how they had all the important things in common.

And as much as any of that, I loved how they looked at me. And touched me.

The piece of paper I'd been holding in my hand caught in the breeze, and I jumped to run after it. I'd not wanted to look at it, but knew I had to. It was titled:

Withdrawing from Wellshire University

The words blurred, but I wiped the tears from my eyes. I had to see what Abalone had thrust in my hand after I'd signed her horrible document.

Basically, I had a week to finish up my business with the university. That meant notifying my professors, handing in any schoolwork I wanted to, and surrendering my ID badge. All my courses would get a *W* on my report card, and that would be part of my permanent record. No further details would be shared.

Nice of them.

There really wasn't much to do except quietly disappear. That's what they always wanted people like me to do.

Don't play by everyone else's rules? Well, we're going to teach you a lesson.

Maybe Wellshire wasn't the place for me.

But the arms of the guys might be.

39

CHASE

I was so proud of my girl.

Saddened by her, but also proud.

The day's French class was just wrapping up, and I was blown away at how quickly she was picking up the basics we'd covered. She'd even explained some tricky verb conjugations to the rest of the class in answer to a question I'd asked.

She was studying her butt off. I liked that.

But there was something off about her. As if her usual light was missing. I wasn't surprised. Balancing school and work was a challenge for anyone, even someone as outstanding as she was. But more importantly, she'd made a tough decision about us guys. I wasn't happy about it—none of us were—but we respected *it* just like we respected her. We wanted the best for her and hoped she'd continue to be in our lives in whatever sort of way she was comfortable.

But that didn't mean she didn't show up in my dreams on a regular basis, usually leaving me waking up with a raging hard on.

I was afraid I knew what was really weighing on her. But I wasn't going to bring up the school newspaper article I'd read that morning until she was ready to talk about it.

But fuck. I wish I could take away some of the pain I saw in her eyes. I'd carry it for her. All of it, if I could.

She let out a big sigh when she approached my desk, the other students filtering out to get on with their days. Like always, she was stunning in her simple, tight black jeans and V-neck T-shirt, accented by a bunch of silver chains that lent the badass look that drove me so crazy about her.

"You have time for a sandwich?" I asked her.

She looked up at me with a hint of melancholy. I was going to get to the bottom of what was going on for her.

"Yes, let's do it," she said, brightening up a bit.

We walked to the student union deli, mostly in silence, each of us making small talk about the weather, the blooming flowers, and how the marching band practicing in the distance needed a bit more work before they were ready for prime time.

With our bag of sandwiches and sodas, we settled under a tree away from the crowds.

"How are you?" she asked, with feigned cheer.

I didn't want to make her feel worse than she already seemed, so I kept my thoughts about her turning down a relationship with us three guys to myself.

Well, I'd keep it to myself for now.

"I've got some news to share, Senna," I started.

Her eyebrows rose. "You do?"

"Yeah… since it looks like it's not too likely I'll get a full-time gig at the university here, I've had to seriously consider doing something else."

She stirred the ice in her soda, nodding. "What about that thing you were supposed to translate for the department head?"

"I finished it. But she's still not hooking me up with anything permanent. She just hung that over my head. I think she was full of shit all along."

She pressed her lips together and shook her head slowly. "Horrible. I'm sorry."

I raised my hands like a *stop* sign. "It's not so bad. I'm going to work in the bar Jamie's opening."

Her head whipped in my direction. "He decided to do it after all. Oh my god. Wow. That's so cool."

I reached my fingers toward hers. I needed to touch her one last time.

To my delight, she wrapped hers around mine, and gave me a small smile.

"I'm happy with the decision," I continued. "I can always tutor French if I want to keep my foot in that world."

I lay back and watched the clouds. We all had choices we could make. We might not always like the ones that are available to us, but we had them.

"So, you have something on your mind, Senna," I said, continuing to look up at the sky. I wanted to give her some space to come to me.

"I do. So many things."

I ran my finger over her arm, warm from the sun.

"Today was the last day you'll see me in French class."

I bolted upright. "*What?*"

"I'm leaving the university."

Jesus fucking Christ.

When I could finally speak again, I struggled to string together a coherent sentence. "Wha… no. Tell me. What the hell is going on?"

I turned her face toward mine.

"I met with my advisor today. Because of the newspaper article that came out, and the fact that she basically already hated me, she suggested I withdraw from the university before they kicked me out."

There it was. And what was weighing on my girl was worse than a shit ton of bricks.

That crazy woman had humiliated Senna for the last time.

"And she mentioned my being with Benno, which I

guess is not so much of an issue now." She laughed weakly and shrugged.

"Senna, look at me. She cannot do that. No one can make you leave. She's full of shit. Fuck this."

I grabbed my phone and texted Benno and Jamie. We were getting together the minute they finished the day's classes. This would only stand over my dead body.

"It's okay, Chase. Don't get involved. None of you should. She'll find a way to hurt each one of you."

I hit *send* on my text. "No. I don't think so. Nor do I care."

I waited for a reply from the guys. It took less than a minute.

"Senna, the guys want to meet tonight at Jamie's condo. Will you come?"

"Are you sure? I mean, do you really want to get involved?" she asked.

I could swear some of the light was coming back to her eyes. She was smart enough to know not to get her hopes up. But she could feel our strength and support. Hopefully, it would help sustain her.

She looked down, nodding, and a couple tears fell onto her lap. "Thank you, Chase. Thank you."

40

CHASE

To my surprise, there wasn't a lot to discuss when we arrived at Jamie's. My brief text had brought Benno up to speed, who had already called in the troops.

We sat around Jamie's spacious living room with cocktails in our hands. We knew things were far from being a done deal, but with the progress Benno had made, we were well on our way to celebrating.

"Where's Senna?" Jamie asked, looking at his watch. "Shit, I hope she's not ghosting us."

God, I hoped not, too. But if she didn't want our help, it was her prerogative. She was free to make the decisions she wanted.

But I sure as hell hoped she'd let us join her in the

battle she faced. There was nothing more that I hated than someone fucking over the underdog.

"I don't get where that woman got off with pressuring Senna to withdraw. Is she fucking out of her mind?" I said.

Benno rubbed his hand over his face. "She's a piece of work. I've been putting up with her craziness for too long. Now it's time to get rid of her. I think we finally have a solid case to make to the administration."

"Think about how many other students she's done this to," Jamie said, shaking his head.

"I don't want to. It's horrifying," Benno agreed.

Jamie jumped to answer his ringing doorbell.

When he returned, Senna was following him, beautiful as always, boldly holding her head up in the face of an ugly situation. She took a seat on the sofa next to me, and I grabbed her hand, bringing it to my lips to kiss the back of it. We might not be lovers any longer, but I wanted her to know how much I cared.

"Hey, darlin'," Benno said, coming over and kissing her cheek.

She smiled wanly. "Hi, guys."

"Sounds like you had kind of a shit day, huh?" Jamie asked.

"I've had better," she said with a laugh.

"I'm sorry—we're all sorry—you're going through this. It's not fair, it's bullshit, and we're putting a stop to it."

Senna frowned. "But, Chase, what can you do? What can any of you do?"

Jamie and I turned our focus to Benno.

"We're going to bat for you, honey. Did you ever doubt that we would?" he asked.

Senna's eyes filled with tears. "Thank you. Thank you, all of you."

I squeezed her hand.

"We're here for you, baby," I said.

Benno continued. "I've briefed the university provost on this situation. You have a meeting with him tomorrow at nine a.m. Can you make that?"

"Sure. It's not like I have classes to attend," she said cynically.

Couldn't blame her.

"This will be taken care of. You are *not* leaving school," he added. "At least not until you are ready to."

She looked at each of us, one by one. "I knew I could count on you."

She leaned toward me and planted a kiss on my lips. Then she got up and did the same to Jamie and Benno.

We looked at each other, wondering what was up. Only a few days before she'd called things off. There was to be no relationship between her and the three of us. It had torn me up, truth be told, but I got it. If it didn't work for her, it didn't work for any of us.

"Oooh, that was a sweet kiss," Jamie said. "I'm gonna miss them."

Now standing in the middle of the room,

surrounded by us, she turned toward him. "Maybe you don't have to miss my kisses."

Huh?

Benno took his glasses off. "What do you mean, Senna?"

She looked at him, then turned to me. "Do *you* know what I'm saying, Chase?" she asked flirtatiously.

"Lay it out for us, baby," I said, hoping she was getting at what I thought she might be.

"After a lot of thought, very careful thought," she said, looking at each of us, "I realized how much I wanted to be with you. *All* of you."

Holy shit. I jumped to my feet, grabbing her and swinging her around.

"Hey, put me down," she squealed, laughing.

Benno, always the cautious one of us three, looked confused. "I thought... I mean... "

"Stop thinking so hard, Professor Adler!"

Benno and Jamie stood up, and we all high-fived each other while we took turns embracing our beautiful girl.

Our girl. She was staying with us. And if we had anything to say about it, she'd stay with the university, too.

41

SENNA

CRAP. I'D NEVER MET WITH A PROVOST BEFORE.

Hell, if I were honest, I wasn't even sure what a provost *was*. But he was obviously a big deal. Not to mention kind for being willing to listen to my situation.

Or was he going to be as horrid as Krishelle Abalone?

No way. Benno would never send me into another lion's den.

I got to Dr. Gilpin's office early in case there was bad traffic or, I don't know, the earth broke open and tried to swallow me up. But, so as to not look desperate or pathetic, I waited in the hallway until three minutes before our nine a.m. meeting.

I wasn't sure what this man could do for me since I'd already signed the withdrawal papers, and I had no doubt Abalone had run to whatever office processed them so she could get rid of me as fast as possible.

It was all pretty incredible how this woman had it out for me. I mean, what the fuck did I ever do?

Actually, I knew I'd done nothing. She was a psycho, and I just happened to be available for her to torment. Next semester it would be a new student, and she'd shit all over them.

But even if Gilpin couldn't do a damn thing for me and I was never to set foot on the Wellshire campus again, I'd come out on top, anyway. I had Benno, Jamie, and Chase by my side, and with them, I could handle anything that came my way.

Well, I could handle my shit before they came on the scene, but it was nice for three hot dudes to have my back.

I rapped on Dr. Gilpin's door and a muffled voice hollered for me to come in.

I walked up to him with my hand extended. "Dr. Gilpin, I'm Senna Duncan. Thank you for seeing me."

He was a disheveled man with kind, blue eyes and a pink face. He must have been a good fifteen to twenty years older than Benno, who'd explained that people usually taught for many years before joining a school's administration. So I guess the man had spent a lot of time in the classroom in preparation for helping to run the university.

I scanned his office for a hint of what he might have taught before becoming a provost. It was hard to tell. All he had on his walls were photos of former administrators and a world map.

"Thanks for coming in, Senna. I'm sorry to hear you're going through such a rough time."

Shit. His kind words made my eyes well, but I willed myself not to cry. I didn't know whether it was from relief that this person seemed like a nice guy, or if something paternal about him made me miss having my own dad.

I often wondered how my life would have turned out if Dad hadn't run next door to 'help out' the man who'd occasionally borrowed his lawn mower and whom he always waved to when he was coming and going.

You just never knew what you were stepping into.

I remembered when it happened, when the gun fired. My mom ran next door and all I could hear was her screaming. Even though I was only ten, I knew to call 911 and give them my name and address. When the police arrived, they told me I'd been very brave and that they admired me for handling the call.

That was when I started handling everything in my life. My ten year old self was suddenly promoted to someone who had the responsibility of an adult, as my mother took to the couch, where she was probably lying at this very moment on this very day.

So after essentially bringing myself up, I figured I was ready for most anything. But navigating a university was about as foreign to me as anything I'd ever known. Maybe I wasn't cut out for college, just like my mother had always told me.

"All right Senna, Professor Adler, who is a friend of mine, let me know you've had problems with a certain administrator, Krishelle Abalone."

I nodded. "Yes, that's true."

"And that she pressured you to withdraw from the university, even though you are receiving exemplary grades and haven't missed a single class?"

"Yes."

I wondered how much he knew.

Oh, fuck it. If he didn't know everything, he deserved to.

"You see, she found out, via the school newspaper, that I have a job as a dancer at an adult club, and told me it was best that I left before I got kicked out."

He shook his head slightly, looking puzzled. "Did she say *why* you would be expelled?"

"Essentially, she said I'd bring shame on the university if it got out."

He looked down at his notes and rubbed his hand through his sparse hair. "Jesus."

What did he mean? 'Jesus' that I was a go-go dancer? Or 'Jesus' that Abalone was full of shit?

"Do you know how the story ended up in the paper?" he asked.

"Yes, I do."

I told him the whole story of Ty extorting me for dates and such. I even told him I wrote one of his papers to get rid of him, but that nothing had worked.

Dr. Gilpin shook his head in disbelief.

"I'm sorry that happened to you. Would you be willing to put all that down in a written statement? We need to address Ty's behavior as well as Abalone's. And there will be some discussion of your writing another student's paper, but we'll take care of first things first."

"Of course I will. Thank you. Do you know what my penalty will be for writing Ty's paper?"

He tilted his head. "It's usually pretty severe. But given the circumstances, that you were basically pressured at the risk of losing so much, I think I can talk to the other administrators I'll be discussing this with. They may be willing to drop this. As long as you *never* do it again."

Sounded like he was assuming I'd get to stick around.

He took a deep breath and pulled from the bottom of a pile of papers the very withdrawal documents I'd signed the day before.

Jesus. Benno and he hadn't wasted any time.

"Senna, I can tell you, unequivocally, that the

university is honored to have a student like you enrolled."

What did he just say? Honored? The university was honored? To have *me*?

"Um, really?" I said in a small voice.

Damn tears were threatening again.

"It's not every day I see a student who has worked as hard as you to get here, and to remain here. If anything, we need a lot more students like you."

Was he kidding? Was this some sort of joke?

"And what you do to support yourself, and to cover your tuition, is nobody's goddamn business. I have a meeting with Ms. Abalone later today and will be addressing this with her."

Okay, there went a tear, right down my cheek, in front of this provost dude who I'd only just met.

"Thank you," I croaked.

"One other thing."

Shit. I'd been waiting for this.

"Benno let me know he's been seeing you socially, outside of class. That, too, is nobody's business. The university doesn't like it because it can leave the student vulnerable, but in this case, I'd say you have the maturity to handle it."

Holy shit.

"I have your withdrawal papers right here. Would you like to tear them up? Or do you really want to leave Wellshire?"

I broke out in a smile, with a little sniffling from my

almost-cry, and lunged for the papers. I glanced at them briefly and noted the spot where I'd signed my name right next to Abalone's. I made sure to tear the paper right through her signature.

Take that, you nasty woman.

42

SENNA

I NEARLY SKIPPED ACROSS CAMPUS, BOTH THRILLED AND humbled that I'd received such strong support from Dr. Gilpin.

I belonged.

I belonged here. Everything the school had to offer was mine for the taking if I wanted it. I was just as entitled as every other student on campus and deserved to be here as much as anybody else did.

It was funny, but his undoing the garbage Abalone had been shoving down my throat since day one made me lighter. I could *do* this.

I slipped into Jamie's math class just before he closed the door to start his lecture.

"Glad you could make it, Miss Duncan," he said with a half-smile.

Shit, I hope no one else had seen that.

"So am I, Professor Carter."

As happy as I was to be in his class, I barely paid any attention to his lesson, my mind flooded with all the opportunity the school offered now that the kind words of Dr. Gilpin had relieved me of a huge burden.

When class ended, I was still doodling in my notebook.

"Senna, did you hear a single thing I said in the last hour?" he asked after the last student had gone.

I jumped up from my seat and ran to him. "I'm sorry, Jamie. I just had the most amazing meeting with the provost. He's going to take care of everything with Abalone. He told me the university's lucky to have a student like me. Can you believe it?"

I thought about pinching myself to make sure I was really awake.

Jamie threw his arms around me. "That's great news, baby. We have so much to celebrate."

"What do you mean? Is there something else going on?" I asked.

"Yeah," he said, shaking his head and smiling. "The department head, who I thought hated me, is nominating me for a full professorship."

"Oh my god!" I screamed and threw my arms around him again.

Then I stepped back. "Wait. Does that mean you're

not opening the bar? I thought you'd signed a lease and everything."

"I am. And I have," he laughed. "I am still opening the bar. In fact, I was heading over there now to meet with the architect. You want to come with? Benno and Chase are meeting me there."

No need to twist my arm.

"I'd love to come. That way I can share the good news with them, too."

Holy crap. It was amazing how one day your life could be circling the drain, but the next gave you the opportunity to not only recover, but potentially soar.

Those were the opportunities you had to grab, quickly, before they were gone.

After a drive that didn't even take ten minutes, we arrived at a nondescript storefront that looked like it had been abandoned for years.

"Wow. What used to be here?" I asked, wondering if Jamie had been taken. The place was a mess.

"Not positive," he said, getting out of the car. "But I think it may have been a drug store."

Jesus, it would cost a small fortune to turn this shell of a building into something warm and welcoming where people wanted to hang out. But that seemed to be no problem for Jamie's budget. More power to him. He was putting his money to good use, creating jobs and cleaning up blight on the street.

"Hi, guys," I said, running to Benno and Chase, greeting each with big hugs and kisses.

"Senna has good news, guys," Jamie said.

They just smiled. Did they already know?

I clapped my hands together gleefully. "Dr. Gilpin was awesome. So kind and understanding. I'm just blown away." Once again, I tried not to choke up.

How did I get so freaking lucky?

"That's awesome baby," Chase said, picking me up and twirling me around.

"Oh, guys," I said breathlessly. "I'm so happy. I feel like I won the lottery. And looks like Jamie is getting his full professorship."

"Hey, if you're still going to teach, who will run the bar?" I asked him.

He took a deep breath and looked at Chase. "I was kind of hoping my friend here might be interested."

Chase broke out in a huge smile and high-fived Jamie. "Fuck yeah, I'd love to run your place." He extended his hand, and Jamie shook on it. "And maybe our girl here would like to help me run it. On a part-time basis of course, as schoolwork allows."

Holy crap. What a great idea. "Oh my god, I'd love to."

"I'll teach you to tend bar. If the business takes off, you'll make way more money than you can at Club V," he added.

Leaving Club V... that wouldn't be easy. But maybe it was time?

"Oh, hey," Benno said. "I'm not supposed to say

anything, but it will be public very soon anyway. Gilpin had Krishelle Abalone fired."

Oh, thank god.

We headed toward Jamie's building to see what the architect had in mind for him.

Chase slapped Benno on the back. "Oh no. What is the sexiest professor in the West going to do without his stalker?"

"Jesus Christ, Chase. Drop it," Benno complained.

With Chase and Benno continuing to bicker, and Jamie laughing, I watched my three guys pass through the future bar's door, opening a new chapter in all our lives.

43

BENNO

I owed my friend Gilpin a bottle of scotch for getting Senna all straightened out. He'd intercepted her withdrawal papers before they'd been put in the system, so she didn't even have to be reinstated.

I wasn't sure what I would have done if she'd left the university. If she wasn't going to be seeing us guys *and* wasn't going to be taking classes, it would have been over between us. I just couldn't imagine any scenario where I or any of the other guys would have a chance to see her on a regular basis.

In fact, we'd probably never see her.

But a week later, it was like nothing had ever

happened besides a small hiccup that was quickly and cleanly overcome. She was back in her classes. Even better, she wanted to keep seeing us. It felt pretty fucking good.

In fact, in class, I could barely keep my hard dick under control just looking at her sitting there at her desk, paying close attention and taking notes like the little angel that she was. Every now and then she'd give me her little half smile, crossing and uncrossing her legs. Of course she was doing it just to torment me. She knew well the effect it was having because I avoided getting up from my desk the entire class.

I'd get even with her later, though.

She sauntered up to my desk after the classroom had cleared. "I noticed Ty was missing."

I stuffed my things into my satchel and slung it over my shoulder. "Yeah. He won't be back."

Her eyes widened. "What happened? Can you tell me?"

"I'm not supposed to. But I will. He's been expelled from the university for cheating and sexual harassment."

The kid had thrown away opportunities other people would kill for.

"Wow. Just wow," she said as I ushered her into the crowded hallway.

"Your statement put the seal on the deal. Apparently, he'd pulled some other shit. The athletic director wasn't happy but acknowledged he couldn't turn his back on it this time. It would blow up into a scandal of epic proportion if it got out that the university knew this was going on and did nothing."

She nodded, absorbing the news.

"It's a shame. He ruined a sweet ride. All he had to do was behave, but he couldn't even manage that," I said as we dodged people in the crowded hallway.

"It is kind of sad. I mean, on one hand I'm very glad he's out of my hair, but on the other, I do hold some compassion for him."

That's what I loved about our girl. Always had room for kindness.

"Hey, what time are the festivities tonight?" she asked.

"We're meeting at the building at eight."

"Does the bar have a name yet?" she asked.

"Yeah. He let Chase name it since he'll be running it. He chose *Rendezvous*."

What else would a French teacher choose?

A few hours later I met the guys at Jamie's new establishment. It was still an eyesore from the street, but when I walked in, I saw he'd transformed it into a sort of charming, festive construction zone.

"Whoa. How did you do all this?" I asked, doing a three-sixty to take it all in. Christ, I'd been afraid the ceiling might fall in on all of us.

The former drugstore, once littered with the debris

of crumbling walls and old, collapsed shelves and other flotsam and jetsam, had been cleared out and cleaned to the best extent possible. There was a makeshift bar set up on one side, and a few bistro tables and chairs scattered about. What made it work without looking like a pathetic attempt to put lipstick on a pig were the strings of lights hanging from the ceiling and draped across the room to look like a sky full of stars.

It was perfect for a little pre-construction ground-breaking celebration.

And then our Senna arrived, in a low-cut dress with a very fitted top and a flared skirt, making her look like a damn 1950's pin-up star.

"Hello, gentlemen," she smiled, stepping carefully on the uneven foundation.

We couldn't take our eyes off her.

It was freaking remarkable that what started as a semester I was dreading turned into something so different than what I—or anyone—expected. Just goes to show, you never know what lies ahead.

After Senna greeted Jamie and Chase, I pulled her to me, inhaling her clean scent and stealing a quick squeeze of her round bottom.

She put her hands on either side of my face and pressed her lips to mine.

When she pulled away, she gave me a naughty smile. My dick jumped to attention, like it always did. "Wanna hear a secret?"

I ran my fingers through her hair. "Hmmm. Not sure."

"Well, I'm telling you, anyway. The night I danced for you at Club V?"

Like I could fucking ever forget that.

"What about it?"

She giggled. "I wasn't supposed to dance for you. Zin had told me there was a birthday boy in the group and asked me to pay special attention to him. But I got you guys mixed up. I gave you the dance instead of him."

"I figured that when you whispered 'happy birthday' in my ear. Poor guy missed out on his birthday gift," I said, laughing. Lucky me, though.

Who knew what lay ahead for any of us, but I knew that with Senna in our little circle, things would never be dull, and would most likely always find a way to work themselves out in the most unexpected way possible.

I mean, who the hell knew I'd find Senna Duncan in my Freshman English class?

Did you like *Her Dirty Teachers?*
Learn about the next HOT story in the Men at Work
Series,
Her Dirty Doctors

I hope you loved reading this book as much as I loved writing it. Please visit my store to learn more about my books, and to buy directly from me!
https://mikalaneshop.com/

ABOUT THE AUTHOR

Dear Reader:

I'm USA TODAY bestselling romance author Mika Lane, and am OBSESSED with bringing you sassy, steamy stories with imperfect heroines and the bad-a*s dudes they bring to their knees. I'll always bring you my signature humor and heat, topped off with a modern-day happily ever after.

My first book ever was *The Day I Ate the Milkyway*, a true fourth-grade masterpiece illustrated with crayons and bound with construction paper and glue. Nowadays, steamy romance gives purpose to my days and nights as I create worlds and characters that tickle the imagination. I live in magical Northern California with my own handsome alpha dude, sometimes known as Mr. Mika Lane, and two devilish cats named Chuck and Murray.

A dual citizen of the United States and Ireland, I have on more than one occasion spent my last dollar on a plane ticket somewhere, and am always planning my next escape. I often try new recipes on unsuspecting friends, search out hiding places to read undisturbed, and sadly kill every houseplant I bring home.

I LOVE to hear from readers when I'm not dreaming up naughty tales to share. Visit my online shop https://mikalaneshop.com/ and say hello https://mikalaneshop.com/pages/meet-mika.

xoxo, Mika